'What the *hell?*'

Drake O'Keefe dropped [...]
several times, then sq[...]
'She jumped. I can't believe she jumped. What is she? Nuts?'

He'd been keeping an eye on the big yacht for the past hour. Obviously a wedding. He hoped they weren't planning to honeymoon on his island.

'Man, that must have been some lovers' quarrel,' Drake muttered to himself. He'd seen the bride's struggle with her dress and then her jump, with her veil trailing after her like a comet's tail. Drake watched the churning froth of white until he noticed the bride's head bob to the surface. She didn't look as if she was doing all that well, but at least she— 'No, you moron!'

The groom had finally decided to help his erstwhile bride. A life preserver sailed through the air, hitting her on the head. Drake was concentrating so intently on the woman that several seconds passed before he realized the yacht was sailing off.

'Hey!' Drake actually stood and waved both arms above his head. 'Get back here! Your bride's overboard!'

For Elaine Galit
in appreciation for all her support

'I've always been intrigued by the premise of the runaway bride or groom,' says **Heather MacAllister**. '*Jilt Trip*, my first Temptation® novel, was part of the GROOMS ON THE RUN mini-series. I had so much fun writing that story that I was thrilled to hear that Temptation had decided to reverse the roles and have the brides running for a change. Of course, my bride doesn't actually *run*, but she does make a spectacular escape—right into the arms of Drake, my version of Cary Grant in *Father Goose*.' In May 1998, look for Heather's next book in Mills & Boon Enchanted® entitled *Marry in Haste*, written under the name of **Heather Allison**.

HEATHER MacALLISTER is also the author of the following books in *Temptation*:

JILT TRIP
BEDDED BLISS
CHRISTMAS MALE

BRIDE OVERBOARD

BY

HEATHER MacALLISTER

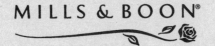

MILLS & BOON®

*MILLS & BOON and MILLS & BOON with the Rose Device
are registered trademarks of the publisher.
TEMPTATION is a registered trademark of
Harlequin Enterprises Limited, used under licence.*

*First published in Great Britain 1998
by Harlequin Mills & Boon Limited,
Eton House, 18-24 Paradise Road, Richmond, Surrey TW9 1SR*

© Heather W. MacAllister 1997

ISBN 0 263 80812 2

21-9803

*Printed and bound in Great Britain
by Caledonian International Book Manufacturing Ltd, Glasgow*

1

TWITCHING HER VEIL aside so she could read, Blair Thomason opened her day planner and ran down the final wedding checklist. *Flowers*. Check. *Musicians*. She opened the door to the master stateroom of the *Salty Señorita*, listened to the flamenco guitarist and winced. Perhaps she could persuade the mariachist—mariachi man?—player?—to refrain during the wedding processional. Making a note beside *musicians*, she continued checking off various bridal elements until she reached the last thing on her list: groom. With a huge smile of satisfaction, she checked off Armand's name—all of it.

At precisely 8:17, as the setting sun cast its golden glow over the Gulf of Mexico, Blair would become Mrs. Armand Luis Jorge de Moura lo Santro Y Chiapis-Chicas Y Barrantes. Or was that Chicas-Chiapis? Blair made a note. Armand rarely used his full name, and when Blair asked him why there was so much of it, he vaguely alluded to a royal quarrel in his family history.

Royalty. Blair sighed. Armand could trace his lineage back hundreds of years. Armand had roots and by grafting herself onto his family tree, Blair would have roots, too.

There was a tap on the stateroom door. "Blair, my darling?"

"Armand!" Blair propped herself against the door. "You know it's bad luck to see the bride before the ceremony."

A richly accented chuckle sounded in the galleyway. "I saw you when we boarded this afternoon. I watched and admired as you most capably directed the catering staff."

Blair smiled at his praise. She'd hoped he'd noticed because she suspected hostessing elegant entertainments would be one of her future responsibilities as Armand's wife. "But I wasn't officially a bride yet. I didn't have on my wedding dress."

"My darling, you needn't have gone to so much trouble. This is merely the civil ceremony. In Argentina, we will be married in the de Moura family chapel by the priest who baptized me. You will wear the lace mantilla that generations of de Moura brides have worn before you."

As his words painted a future she desired with all her heart, Blair clutched her day planner to her chest and shivered. *Generations. Family.* She sighed, almost able to forget that none of Armand's extended family was present to witness the ceremony today. But she had no family present, either, and no friend close enough to ask to make the trip to Argentina with her.

"I will not have my bride touched by the fetid breath of scandal," Armand had declared. "Since you have no female traveling companion, we shall journey to Argentina cloaked in civil respectability."

Blair wondered if there was going to be a civil honeymoon as well as a religious one. She and Armand had not yet...well, Armand was very conscious of her honor. She would be able to face his family pure in heart, if not in actual fact.

"My darling," he said, "one of my cuff links has broken and I would like to retrieve another pair from the safe in the stateroom."

"Is everyone in the salon?" Blair asked.

"I believe so."

"Good. Then I'll be able to slip out and check on things one more time. Turn your back," she instructed.

When she opened the door, Armand, his dark hair just brushing his collar, stood with his back to her, as she'd known he would. Armand was a man of honor.

She was so very lucky, Blair thought, gathering the train of her dress over her arm and climbing to the upper deck. Though neither of Blair's parents would come to see their daughter married, Armand had not even raised an eyebrow in disapproval. He'd simply suggested an early civil ceremony to avoid any implications of impropriety.

Blair felt cherished for the first time in her life. Someone cared about her. Someone cared *for* her.

Unbidden, her mother's off-repeated advice drifted through her mind, "The first time marry for money. Then you can afford to marry for love. I got it backward and look what happened to me." Actually, Blair's mother had been married so many times, Blair couldn't remember if her current husband was love or money.

She reached the upper deck and surveyed the scene with satisfaction. It might be a civil ceremony, but a wedding was a wedding and Blair wanted it to feel like one. She needed the familiar bridal trappings to feel anchored to reality.

Anchored. She grinned. Six weeks ago she'd been an efficiency analyst with Watson and Watson Management Consultants in Houston. Now she was about to become the wife of Armand de Moura lo Santro y…etcetera. She really must remember the order. She'd actually written it down both ways.

Such sloppiness wasn't like her, but planning a wedding and preparing to live in another country all in two weeks had taxed even her organizational abilities.

Blair straightened a row of white folding chairs. Armand and his friends noticed details like crooked rows. She tugged on the white satin runner and refastened it. Two bouquets of white roses stood on either side of an arched trellis.

Blair frowned. The trellis, festooned with a huge white bow, didn't look quite right on the ship and it blocked the view of the sunset. The streamers from the bow flapped in the wind, which was much stronger than it had been earlier.

That's it. The trellis goes. Ugly silver duct tape secured the base to the deck. Blair peeled it away to find that a sticky residue marred the varnished surface. Oh, well, she'd position the justice of the peace there.

Once released, the trellis wobbled in the breeze. Now where was she supposed to put it? No one was around to help her. The guests, Armand's usual cadre of friends, would be in the salon eating canapés. The two-man crew had been pressed into service as waiters. The musicians were still below. Great.

She could not deal with her train, her veil *and* the trellis, so Blair simply lifted the construction over the railing and let the wind do the rest.

The trellis landed in the gulf, bobbing in the *Salty Señorita*'s wake.

Much better. Blair gazed out at the horizon. On the left, the Texas-Mexico coastline smudged into the edge of the ocean. Oil-drilling platforms spoiled the beauty, which was why the *Salty Señorita* was sailing so far out. Blair wanted nothing to mar her photographic memories.

She watched the trellis, a bright white against the muddy waters, and waited for it to sink. Her veil whipped across her face, stinging her eyes. This wind was really something. She'd have to check her makeup and figure out a way to fasten her veil, so it wouldn't go flying off during the ceremony.

Just as Blair turned to go below, a shape appeared from between the jumble of oil rigs and coastline. A boat. A small, ugly boat. Since it was ahead of them and traveling the same path, it was bound to be in the pictures, she thought ruefully. The ceremony was due to begin in twenty-two minutes. If the boat continued on course, it would be smack-dab in the middle of the horizon, a blot marring the matrimonial perfection she'd planned.

She couldn't have that.

Avoiding the salon, she returned to the master stateroom, half hoping to find Armand.

It was empty.

Blair retouched her makeup and pinned her veil tightly, using so many bobby pins that the only way it was coming loose was if she was scalped.

Satisfied, she grabbed her day planner in case she needed to alter the timetable, and made her way to the pilothouse. She wanted to ask the captain to change course or hail that stupid boat and tell it to get out of the way.

Armand's dark head was visible through the open doorway. Maybe he'd noticed the boat and was conferring with the captain.

It would be just like Armand. He, too, was a detail-oriented person. That was why they got along so well together.

Blair, careful to keep her dress from touching any of the equipment bolted to the deck, edged forward, trying to hear but also trying to stay out of Armand's sight.

"—long until we're in Mexican waters?" he was asking.

"Not for another forty minutes," the captain replied.

"Perhaps you could go a little faster?" Armand suggested.

"It'll get mighty breezy up on that top deck."

"That is not my concern. My only concern is that we are in Mexico before the justice of the peace pronounces us man and wife."

"I'll see what I can do, sir." The pitch of the engines climbed.

Mexico. They were scheduled to stop for the night at the resort town of Sonoma Villa where they'd bid farewell to their guests and presumably begin their honeymoon.

Blair smiled. Armand must be rattled. It wasn't like him to make such a mistake. He meant to inform the captain that they should *not* be in Mexican waters when the Texas justice of the peace performed the ceremony. The JP wouldn't have jurisdiction in Mexico. Their marriage wouldn't be legal.

She took two steps toward the pilothouse, then stopped. Armand hadn't sounded rattled, though she saw him check his pocket watch.

"Do you think that boat belongs to the United States authorities?" he asked.

Feeling uneasy, Blair stepped into a stairwell and stayed out of sight.

"As far as I can tell, it's a lone fisherman," the captain replied.

"What is he doing?"

"It appears that he's watching us as closely as we're watching him."

"I don't like it." Armand's tone, while still accented, was clipped and devoid of the charming drawl with which he usually spoke.

"No one has reason to suspect anything. You staged the ceremony right out in the open—which is a nice touch, I might add. If this fisherman is with some law-enforcement agency, then he'll see a wedding as announced."

Blair stopped breathing. *Law?*

"Don't worry, Señor Varga. As usual, all is superbly planned."

Varga? The captain had called Armand Señor Varga. Blair might not be sure of the precise order of all Armand's names, but she knew which ones were there and which ones weren't. Varga wasn't. Was it?

Flipping open her day planner, she turned to the copy of the announcement she'd sent to the newspaper before she left. Armand Luis…it *was* Chiapis-Chicas, she noted—but there was no Varga.

Blair shook her head. She must have misunderstood. Her life had taken such an unreal turn so quickly that her mind couldn't absorb everything and had chosen now to malfunction, she told herself.

Blair liked things orderly and she'd been rushed to get ready for this wedding. She thought she'd handled everything, but…

"It's time," Armand announced with a heavy sigh. "If I do not signal the guests that it is time to leave the salon, my efficient bride will. Perhaps I can create a small time-consuming diversion… you will ring the bell when we cross into Mexican waters?"

Blair didn't wait to hear the captain's response. Gathering her train, she ran to the railing on the opposite side of the yacht and stared at the churning wake.

Varga? Law? Mexican waters? Superbly planned *as usual?* He'd done whatever he was doing before? Just how many faux brides were out there struggling to memorize the order of his names?

She could *not* have heard correctly.

She hadn't eaten since breakfast. That was it. She should eat something. Low blood sugar did funny things to the brain.

"Pondering the enormous leap you are about to take, my love?" Armand spoke from just behind her, his drawl in place, though not as charming as Blair remembered.

"Leap?" Blair whipped around, brushing the veil out of her face. "What leap?"

"Marriage," he replied lightly. "A leap of faith."

Apparently blind faith on her part. "Yes, it is a leap, isn't it? Because of you, I'm off to live in a country I don't know, among people I don't know, with a man…" She turned back to stare at the coastline.

"With a man who is grateful you've chosen to do so," Armand smoothly supplied. "You look lovely, my dear," he said, taking a step toward her.

Blair cringed against the railing, her veil billowing.

"Ah. I was not supposed to see you before the ceremony, was I?"

"No."

"My apologies."

She heard him pivot. "Armand?"

"My love?"

"It's so windy and this veil is being such a pain. Would you please tell the captain to slow down. Or better yet—" she turned so she could see his face "—ask him to drop anchor here until after the ceremony?" Blair still clutched her day planner, her train and hope.

The small smile remained fixed in place. Armand's dark eyes gave nothing away. "Such a lot of trouble for a veil. Now, if it were my family's bridal mantilla, that would be understandable."

Blair gave him a brilliantly false smile. "Oh, but Armand, I want everything to be perfect." She linked her arm through his. "Let's go ask the captain together."

He allowed her three steps before she felt resistance.

Blair ignored it. "Oh, look!" She pointed and tugged him along. "That trashy little boat's going to spoil our pictures! We simply must speak to the captain—"

"I think we needn't bother the captain over trivialities, my dear." He patted her hand.

As unobtrusively as she could, Blair disengaged her arm. "Then it's time to direct the guests from the salon to the upper deck," she said. "We've timed everything so carefully. After all," she forced herself to add, "we don't want to leave Texas before we're married."

That's your cue. Laugh and agree. Then I'll know everything will be fine.

Armand didn't move. "Something troubles you, my love. The guests can wait a bit longer."

A small, time-consuming diversion…

Blair wanted to scream. Instead, she gazed at Armand, judging the man she thought she knew against the man she'd overheard. The long rays of the setting sun emphasized the furrows and hollows in his face. His jawline was soft. Bronzed skin from his neck lapped over the edge of his white shirt. Impossibly black hair and a pencil-thin mustache absorbed the light without giving any back.

How old is he? "You're not thirty-seven, are you?" she blurted out.

His face creased as he smiled—with relief, she suspected.

"I am thirty-seven in my heart." He placed both hands over the organ in question.

"So how old are you outside your heart? Forty-seven?" That would make him more than twenty years older than Blair.

At his raised eyebrow and elegant shrug, she felt chilled.

"My darling, I will answer your question, but do you truly wish me to?"

No, she didn't. Besides, she had another. "Are you in trouble with the law?"

She'd surprised him.

His black eyebrows arched, then he regarded her intently. "Someone has said something to you. What?"

Not, "No, what are you talking about?" or "Don't be silly, my darling." Blair's last doubts of his perfidy disappeared along with her dreams.

"No one has said anything," she snapped. "I overheard you talking with the captain. You were concerned that the feds were following you in that junky boat." She flung her arm toward it.

Armand glanced at her consideringly, then moved to stand next to her at the railing. "I could continue to maintain the masquerade by telling you that I was referring to customs officials and that I didn't want our wedding interrupted. But I think that would be pointless, would it not?"

"Pretty much." He'd always had just the right response to her questions. Blair began to see how she'd allowed herself to be manipulated. "And speaking of weddings, I gather that you didn't want our marriage to be legal."

Armand drew a deep breath and leaned against the railing, not looking at her. "I've found that life is so much more flexible without legal entanglements."

Blair paced. She'd been well and truly taken in. Armand was nothing more than a charming crook. "Well...congratulations, Armand," she said, coming to a stop in front of him. "You had me completely fooled. 'Lighten up,' my co-workers had said. 'You're so uptight, Blair,' they said. 'Seize the day. Relax. Be impulsive for once.' So I was impulsive and look where it got me."

Armand cleared his throat. "I hardly think two weeks of meticulous planning is impulsive."

"For me it is," she said dryly.

"My dear, you mustn't blame yourself," he said consolingly. It sounded like a speech he'd given before.

"Oh, I don't," Blair said. "It was a grand and glorious six weeks. You are a charming companion, Armand." She wasn't about to let him—or anyone—see that she'd been hurt.

"As are you." He bowed slightly and offered her his arm. "Come, my dear. It is time for the ceremony."

Blair laughed. "You aren't *that* charming. It won't be legal anyway. And now that I know, what's the point?" She started for her stateroom, yelping when her veil caught on something and pulled her hair.

Her veil had caught on Armand's hand. "The point is that we have guests who expect a wedding. And I want them to see a wedding." He tugged on the veil, causing her to stumble forward. "In particular, I want them to return to their homes and discuss the wedding."

"Why?"

Armand smiled his unctuous smile. "Because they surely do not expect me to conduct business when I am on a wedding journey with such a beautiful bride."

Blair thought of the twenty people accompanying them. Three couples were his "dearest friends" and fellow Argentineans, lovely people who made Blair feel as though she were one of them. Then there was the justice of the peace and his wife, while the others were part of the crowd that had grown around Armand during his stay in Texas, most of whom had invested in his beef-shipping venture. "What possible difference—" Blair asked this just as the answer occurred to her. "The investors—this is a scam, isn't it? There is no Argentinean beef-shipping consortium, is there?"

"There most assuredly is." This time, Armand's smile was one of extreme self-satisfaction.

"But..." Realization dawned. "You're swindling *both* sides, aren't you?" And a bride.

"Double the pleasure, double the fun and double the take," said Armand.

"And I provided you with the perfect cover, didn't I?"

"You are the most efficient woman I have ever met." He bowed over her hand.

Blair snatched it away. "Not so efficient that I saw through you."

Armand looked pained. "I cannot allow you to blame yourself," he repeated. "I am very experienced in these matters."

"So what were you planning to do with me after the wedding?" Blair asked, thinking she should have rephrased her question. "Leave me in Sonoma Villa? I'd awaken after my wedding night and find that my groom had run out on me?"

"Oh, no, my dear. People expect us to be on a wedding journey of some four months." Armand reached out and caressed her cheek. Blair recoiled and he let his hand drop.

"I'm not going anywhere with you for four months."

"I did not say I would be with you."

"You're darn right you're not going to be with me. As soon as we dock in Sonoma Villa, I'm outta here." She snatched her veil out of his hand and marched toward the stateroom, intending to lock herself in.

Armand grabbed her arm. "The ceremony, darling."

She jerked her arm away. "I am *not* going through with that sham. You're going to have to swindle those people without my help."

"Dear girl, you have no choice in the matter. The captain and crew are in my employ."

"So what are they going to do? Hold a gun on me? That'll sure give people something to talk about. And while I'm there, how about I tell everybody just what a crook you are?"

Armand didn't seem particularly bothered by her threat. "Crooks *we* are," he corrected.

"*I* haven't done anything."

Armand studied his nails. "That might be difficult for you to prove."

"Why?"

He shuddered delicately as though revealing his methods were distasteful. "There are documents, affidavits, loan papers and the like all bearing your signature." Smiling sadly, he continued, "It would not look good for you, my dear."

"I read everything I signed. I signed applications for residency, I had my money moved to a bank in Argentina..." Blair trailed off, thinking of the unexpected paperwork she'd encountered. There had been a lot, she remembered thinking.

"Do you read Spanish, dear one?" Armand asked softly.

"No, but I read the English translations."

He smiled.

In a heartbeat, she understood. "Oh no," she groaned and looked skyward. Armand had arranged for the English translations. She'd probably never find out what she'd really signed.

"Blair, I like you. Even in your chagrin, you are admiring my thoroughness, no?"

So help her, she was. What was the matter with her? She was in a hideous position, possible physical danger, her good name was ruined—and yet a part of her admired the way everything had fallen into place for him. Almost everything.

"I think I shall take you with me," Armand said after a moment. "I could make you my protégée. We would work well together." His eyes came as close to sparkling as she'd ever seen them. "Think of it. Planning grand schemes down to the tiniest detail."

"You've got to be kidding."

"Blair, Blair." He took her shoulders. "Cut yourself free from the anchor of morality and soar with me!"

"I don't think so."

The light went out of Armand's eyes and he sighed. "So be it. I must remind you that should you speak of this to anyone, I will have authorities waiting to arrest you the moment we dock in Sonoma Villa."

Blair backed away, nearly tripping over a metal cylinder. She grabbed at it to steady herself. "You think you've thought of everything."

"Because I have." Armand uttered the words with supreme self-confidence.

"I bet you haven't thought of this." Blair dropped her planner and yanked the pull ring on the metal cylinder. A life raft shot through the air, inflating as it fell.

"What are you doing?" Armand cried.

"Improvising." Blair grabbed her planner and climbed over the railing.

"Blair, people like us do not improvise well!"

"Goodbye, Armand." She scrambled down the metal ladder.

She'd counted on surprise to hold Armand immobile for a few seconds. She hadn't counted on her train.

With a very un-Armand-like howl, he grabbed it before it could slither over the railing after her.

It was detachable, held in place by a row of tiny satin-covered buttons. Blair jerked. Armand jerked back. The satin buttons held fast. The *Salty Señorita* sailed farther and farther away from the bobbing life raft.

Armand smiled.

Blair reached for the life preserver and jumped, pushing away from the side of the boat with her feet.

The train ripped free, but not before it shortened her jump. Blair felt the life preserver scrape through her fingers and braced for a watery impact.

The gulf was both harder and colder than she'd expected. The air left her lungs and she swallowed a mouthful of salty water before clamping her lips shut and kicking toward the surface.

Her veil dragged at her like bridal seaweed, but she couldn't rip it off. Blair was further hampered by holding on to her day planner as though it were a lifeline. To her, retaining possession of the details of her life was every bit as important as breathing.

Using the book like a paddle, she finally broke the surface and choked in a breath. Well, improvising certainly looked as though it was going to be a sink-or-swim operation.

Hampered by the slim sheath of her wedding dress, she could hardly tread water, much less swim for the life raft. There was no way she could keep afloat for long.

With her free hand, she tore at the veil, unable

to get the sodden mass off her head and tread water at the same time.

She swallowed another mouthful of seawater, yet started paddling determinedly toward the now-distant raft. Someone called her name. Instinctively turning to look, her vision filled with white an instant before pain exploded in her head and she slipped beneath the cool, dark waters of the gulf.

2

"WHAT THE *HELL*?"

John Drake O'Keefe dropped the binoculars, blinked several times then squinted through them again.

"She jumped. I can't believe she jumped. What is she—nuts?"

He'd been keeping an eye on the big motor yacht for the last hour. The top deck was decorated with white froufrou and folding chairs. Obviously a wedding. He hoped they weren't planning to honeymoon on his island.

In the eight months since he'd moved to Pirate's Hideout, there had been instances of visitors who hadn't heard that the exclusive resort had closed due to hurricane damage and was now privately owned.

From experience, he'd found that it was better if he headed off boats instead of allowing them to dock. People had a tendency to disembark once they'd docked somewhere. It didn't matter what he said, they wanted to get off and have a look around, oohing and aahing at the damage and comparing how the place had looked when they were there last.

The first time it happened, Drake had still retained some vestige of polite, civilized behavior and allowed the folks to poke around. Trouble was, they didn't seem to understand the concept of private ownership. Or rather, they understood that he was now the owner, but they just couldn't accept that he wasn't willing—or able—to serve them a meal or put them up for the night.

Now he sailed out to head them off at the pass.

"Man, that must have been some lover's quarrel," Drake muttered to himself. He'd seen the struggle with the train and the bride's jump, veil trailing after her like a comet's tail. It was a long way to the life raft, too. He wished her luck.

Drake watched the churning froth of white until he saw the bride's head bob up through the surface. She didn't look as if she was doing all that great, but at least she— "No, you moron!"

The groom had let fly with the life preserver and had scored a direct hit almost as soon as the woman surfaced.

Drake stared hard at the ring as it flipped, then floated in the water. He couldn't tell if she was okay or not. He could still see white, which meant she hadn't gone under, but he didn't see her head or arms.

He was concentrating so intently that several seconds passed before he realized the yacht was sailing off. He jerked the binoculars to the railing and saw the groom—he assumed it was the groom—staring at the water, arms spread out across the railing. Then, as if the man knew Drake was watching, he looked directly at him. "Yeah, pal, you've got a problem."

But no alarm sounded. No activity indicated a

rescue. And no rope materialized, attaching the life preserver to the yacht.

"Hey!" Drake actually stood and waved both arms above his head. "You've got a woman in the water! Your bride's overboard—get back here!" The yacht didn't slow down.

Stunned, Drake sat abruptly, expecting any moment to see the yacht turn around. Expecting somebody to jump in after her. Expecting... something.

"I don't believe this. You're crazy! Both of you have lost it. Haven't you ever heard of counseling? People make a nice living dealing with crazies like you. This is *not* my problem, people!" He berated the unknown couple even as he nosed his dinghy toward the life preserver and opened the motor full throttle. "My boat's too small for open water. Who did you think was going to rescue you? Huh? Did you think of that before you jumped, lady?" he yelled. "The motor's going to blow any minute. And if it doesn't, I'll probably capsize and we'll both be in the drink."

Nobody could hear him, but Drake continued to rant and rave, steering with one hand, looking through the binoculars with the other. "I'm going to regret this." He cursed and braced himself as the wake from the yacht slapped his boat.

Miraculously, he rode it out and remained afloat, though an inch of water now sloshed around his feet.

Drake continued to plow toward the white blob, the motor protesting nearly as much as he was. Out of habit, he glanced down at his wrist to see how much time had elapsed since the woman had been beaned with the life preserver.

Tan obliterated all but the faintest outline marking the fifteen years where he'd worn his expensive graduation present. He'd kept the watch out of sentimentality, but timepieces were the first things he'd discarded when he'd come to live at the ruined Pirate's Hideout.

So how long had she been in the water? Two minutes? Three? His heart was getting as much of a workout as the engine. He hoped neither gave out.

Once he passed the protective barrier of his island, Drake bucked the waves of the open gulf. Currents were strong in this area and he'd already adjusted his heading as the woman drifted southward.

"Oh, man." When he got close enough to see her legs floating limply beneath the surface, Drake set aside the binoculars and grimly reviewed everything he knew about CPR.

He cut the motor and drifted the rest of the way toward her. "Hey, lady?" Maybe she was just dazed. He could see her veil, which meant her head had to be above water, didn't it?

Grabbing an oar, Drake maneuvered the boat closer and caught his breath.

The woman's veil had become twisted in the life preserver and its rope, keeping her head just above water. But occasionally, the ocean lapped over her face, so she'd probably inhaled a few snootfuls.

Drake prodded her with his oar, trying to bring her within reach without dislodging the floating ring. When he could, he grasped her arm, carefully sliding her closer. Something else, wedged beneath her neck and the ring, had helped keep her head out of the water, as well. A black book floated free when Drake pulled her toward the dinghy. He fished it out and tossed it into the boat.

"Okay, lady, let's see if your luck's held."

He leaned out as far as he dared and tried to disentangle her veil. When he couldn't, he tried unsuccessfully to pull it off her head. What had she used, superglue?

He placed her hands over the side of the dinghy and held them there to keep her from slipping away. Next he heaved the floating ring into the boat.

"You couldn't be a petite five-footer, could you?" He drew a couple of deep breaths, then began the battle of hauling her into his boat.

She was a good-size girl with some muscle on her. Probably had worked out to get ready for her wedding. Muscle weighed more than fat, which wasn't helping him any.

He wondered why she'd jumped. So help him, if he couldn't revive her, he'd never know.

He didn't care, he just wanted to know.

Drake braced his feet against the weathered wooden side of the dinghy and, with a mighty heave, pulled her most of the way in—at least to the point where gravity was finally on his side.

He fished her leg out and she half slid, half rolled into the boat. She was all caught up in the veil, so Drake had to unroll her before he could attempt to get water out of her lungs.

All the jouncing helped, and water drained out of her mouth. "Atta girl." He moved her arms over her head and pressed her back.

More water. He rolled her over, tilted her head back, checked her mouth for any obstructions, pinched her nostrils and puffed air into her lungs, watching to see if her chest rose and fell. It did, but only once.

"Come on, lady. I've gone to a hell of a lot of trouble here and I'd appreciate it if you'd make an effort to cooperate."

Drake thumped her back, willing water to drain out.

He tried mouth-to-mouth resuscitation again and again. He was feeling light-headed, when she jerked and coughed. Her hands clawed air as she choked, gasped, then rolled over and promptly threw up.

Drake had never been so glad to see anyone throw up in his life. He rubbed her back, his hand trembling.

She continued to cough and gurgle. He sat on the wooden seat and dangled his hands between his knees. A cold sweat covered him.

He'd saved her life. He'd never saved anybody's life before. Lifesaving was exhausting.

When at last the woman drew a shuddering breath and lay still, they both sighed.

She was curled on her side, her eyes shut. Her skin was unnaturally pale and the freckles on her nose stood out. Her dress was a tight white number, or it had been until she'd gone for her bridal swim and had been dragged over the side of his boat. There was a slit up the back that had torn, probably when she'd kicked.

And, though he tried not to be aware of it, the damp material was nearly transparent.

To distract himself, Drake gazed at her head-dress, now sporting an aquatic theme. Twisting his head to one side, he read the yacht's name on the life preserver. *Salty Señorita.* How apt. He grinned for the first time today. Maybe for the first time this week.

The salty *señorita* wrinkled her nose and opened her eyes.

Drake prepared himself for an outpouring of gratitude.

She blinked a couple of times, then grimaced. "Oh, gross!" She sat up and scooted toward the other side of the boat away from the mess. "I feel like garbage."

"You look like garbage," Drake offered. But considering what she'd just been through, she could have looked a lot worse.

She squinted at him. "You're that guy in the boat." Reaching up, she began pulling pins out of her hair.

"Yeah." There were a lot of pins. Drake was fascinated by the movements of her fingers as pin after pin dropped into her lap.

"What took you so long?" she asked. "I almost drowned out there."

"What do I look like, the Coast Guard?" She wasn't acting like somebody who had nearly drowned.

She glanced at him, then at his boat. "No. Definitely not the Coast Guard—'' Breaking off, she coughed.

"Are you going to be okay?" Drake asked, refraining from adding, *since you wouldn't be breathing now if it hadn't been for me.*

Nodding, she visibly swallowed. "Yeah, probably."

"You don't sound all that thrilled at the prospect."

She managed a half smile and resumed pulling out the pins. "Is that your subtle way of asking if I was trying to kill myself?"

Drake had always found half smiles sexy, though why he should think so under these circumstances was beyond him. "Were you?"

"No." Her eyes widened, and she swiveled her head from right to left, looking all around them. "Where are we? Where's Armand?"

Must be the groom. "He sailed off while you were playing bride of the sea." Drake pointed southward where a small speck may or may not have been the *Salty Señorita.*

Blinking, she absorbed this development. For the first time, she noticed the life preserver. "What happened?"

"You jumped, surfaced and, about a second later, were conked on the head by that." Drake toed the ring, still enshrouded in bridal netting.

Her eyes grew wide. "You mean, he tried to kill me?"

"I don't think it was intentional. Hitting you from that distance was a hundred-to-one long shot."

"It would have been a lot easier for him if I'd drowned."

"Oh, I don't know. You look like the type to haunt a guy."

"H-how long was I unconscious?" Her face paled even more.

Watching her carefully, Drake shrugged. "A few minutes."

She blinked at him. Her eyes were blue—the pale blue kind that made the pupils stand out. They'd dilated. "I could have drowned," she whispered through lips that were trembling.

"Hey, don't go into shock on me."

"I could have *drowned*," she repeated, sounding bewildered.

"Well, yes, but you didn't."

"But why? Why didn't I drown?"

Approaching her cautiously, Drake touched her clammy arm. *Oh, great.* He briskly rubbed both of them. "Your veil got caught in the ring and kept your head above water. If the ring had flipped the other way, it would have been a different story." One he shouldn't dwell on.

She shuddered.

"Look, it'll be dark soon and I'd better get us to shore. We've already drifted. Hope there's enough gas," he muttered and fired up the motor.

The woman stared dully at him.

"Put your head down." He pressed her forward, but her skirt was so tight she couldn't spread her knees apart. Drake lengthened the rip at the back of her dress.

She didn't even flinch.

Urging her head down, he increased the engine speed and the boat bounced over the waves.

"How're you doing?" he asked after a few minutes of silence.

"I think I'm going to be sick."

"You probably don't have much left to be sick with."

She groaned and resumed pulling out pins without lifting her head. When her fingers didn't find any more, she flipped the veil over her head and Drake saw why it hadn't come loose. Part of her hair was braided over a plastic ring. She fumbled with the rubber band, then jerked it off, bringing several strands of brown hair with it.

He winced.

At last, she pulled the veil from her head and sat up, finger-combing her hair until it hung in wavy strands to her bare shoulders.

Drake studied her. As far as he could see, her pupils were the same size and the zombie look she'd worn earlier was replaced by a pensive expression.

She stared out at the ocean, bathed in the orangy glow of the setting sun. "Thanks," she said quietly, without looking at him.

He understood. Nearly dying would make a person want to reflect for a time.

"What's your name?" he asked her quietly.

"Blair. Blair *Thomason*." There was an unmistakable emphasis on the last name.

"Is that *Mrs*. Thomason?"

She glanced down at a diamond the size of his thumbnail. "No." Holding out her hand, she wiggled her finger and watched the stone catch the light.

"So, Miss Blair Thomason, what happened? Counseling didn't work out?"

Her gaze swept over him as though she was aware she owed him an explanation yet didn't want to give it. "What's your name?"

He could answer anything. He could be anybody. "Drake," he said, deciding on the truth. Deception took too much effort.

"Well, Drake, it was like this. Armand wasn't the man I thought he was."

How intriguing. This Armand had definitely transgressed. Drake wondered how. Must have been a lulu. "Couldn't you have told him you'd changed your mind?"

"I did, but he wasn't taking no for an answer."

Drake waited, but Blair wasn't inclined to elaborate. He couldn't stand it. "And so you jumped ship in a remote area of the Gulf of Mexico? What the hell were you thinking?"

Her eyes narrowed. "It was important to Armand's plan that there be a wedding ceremony. I made sure there wouldn't be one."

"What are you, some kind of heiress?" He glanced at her hand.

"No." Following his gaze, she looked at the ring, then slipped it off. Drake thought she was going to offer it to him as some sort of payment and was preparing to refuse when she raised her arm and he realized she was going to throw the ring into the ocean.

"Hey!" He grabbed her arm. "If you don't want the ring, I'll take it."

"This diamond is probably as fake as Armand."

"But you don't know that for a fact."

She rolled her eyes, crawled toward his rusty metal toolbox and proceeded to pound and rub the big square diamond against the sharp corners.

Drake shook his head.

Blair tilted the ring toward the waning light and smiled grimly. "Fake," she pronounced, crawling back and handing it to him. "And not even a good one."

Gouges and chips scored the surface of the stone.

"Was he a good one?" Drake asked, handing the ring back to her.

She tossed it overboard, then sat on the wooden seat across from him. "Pardon me?"

"Was your Armand a good fake?"

"Triple-A quality."

"At least you found out in time."

"That's a matter of opinion. Look, can you slow down or make the ride smoother?"

"I wish I could. Running at max for this length of time isn't good for the engine, but I don't want to get caught after dark. Won't be able to find my way home."

Blair was gazing intently at the murky shoreline. "Where are the lights?" she asked suddenly.

"I didn't leave any on. Didn't plan to be out this long."

"No, I mean where are the *lights?* From houses and buildings. Streetlights, that sort of thing."

"There aren't any."

"Why not?"

"Because there aren't any people."

"What do you mean, there aren't any people? Where are you taking me?"

"To that island straight ahead and to the right. I live there."

"Alone?"

Drake nodded. "Just me and the gulls."

She recoiled. "I don't want to go to your island."

"You don't have a choice."

With her hands folded quietly in her lap, Blair tilted her head regally. "I demand that you take me to the nearest police station."

"Sorry. No can do."

"Well, you'd better!"

"Or what? You'll jump overboard? Be my guest... And while you're at it, take this with you." He tossed the life preserver with its attached veil toward her.

She glared at him. "You're as bad as Armand."

Unreasonably stung, he protested, "I am nothing like Armand."

"Yes, you are. All men are. You're all bullies."

Drake was beginning to sympathize with the unknown Armand. "Is this the way you show gratitude? By insulting me? Haven't you ever heard of the custom that the savee's life belongs to the saver?"

"Oh, so *that's* what this is about. It got a little lonely on that island, did it, Drake? And what better love slave than a woman who was left for dead?" She scorched him with a look. "You pervert."

"Love slave? *You?*" Drake laughed. The idea

was so preposterous that he laughed more. In fact, he laughed until he was weak, then had to correct the boat's course.

Blair maintained a frigid silence and held herself with such queenly dignity that it set him off again.

"I believe you've made your point with insulting clarity," she said over his fading chuckles.

"Good." He grinned. "And I'm glad to see you aren't dwelling on what some people might see as an enormous debt to the person who saved their life. In fact, some people might even try to cooperate instead of issuing orders."

Her eyes narrowed. "I should have kept my mouth shut about the engagement ring and just given it to you as payment."

"You'd have done that? You'd give the man who saved your life a worthless piece of glass?"

"I wouldn't have known for certain that it was worthless, and material expressions of gratitude seem important to you."

"What gave you that idea?"

"You tried to keep me from throwing the ring away."

"That's because I thought it was a five-carat diamond. I mean, sentimentality aside, a real diamond that size would have netted you at least enough to pay for your dress."

She looked down at herself and grimaced. "You also asked if I was an heiress. I told you no, but it's obvious that you don't believe me."

Drake opened his mouth, then closed it and concentrated on the approaching shoreline. The woman's brains must have been pickled by salt-water. He'd cut her some slack.

"I'm telling you, I'm not an heiress and I'm not wealthy."

"Congratulations."

"So there is no point in kidnapping me. Please take me to the police and I promise I won't mention anything about your momentary lapse."

Drake's brief amusement had long since faded. "Believe me, it would give me the greatest pleasure to unload you onto somebody else, but I can't. The nearest town is San Verde, on the Mexican border, and it's a three- to four-hour boat trip, depending on the boat. And *this* boat can't make the trip."

That shut her up for a while, at least long enough for Drake to concentrate on the approaching shoreline. He just barely avoided running them onto a sandbar.

They were still south of his dock. He cut the motor's speed and rode parallel to the island, straining to find the marina.

"You don't understand." Blair leaned forward. "Armand is a crook—a swindler. A con man. For all I know, he tried to kill me. I've got to tell the police."

"You can tell them whatever you want, but you're not telling them tonight." She was getting on his nerves. *Really* getting on his nerves. Fortunately, he spotted the dock and pointed the dinghy toward it.

"You want details?"

"Not particularly."

"He ran a scam between people in Texas and

Argentina. That's two countries. He's probably broken all kinds of international laws."

"And you were going to marry this guy?" Drake cut the motor and glided into the dock.

"Not after I found out."

"That would be when you jumped overboard."' He climbed on to the dock.

"Yes."

Blair threw him the rope and he tied the boat to a wooden post with a No Trespassing sign nailed to it.

"Get your stuff," he ordered. "You can clean up the boat tomorrow."

Her mouth dropped open, but amazingly she didn't argue. She grabbed the life preserver and veil and held out her hand.

"Is that planner yours?" Drake pointed. "It was tangled in your veil."

"You found my organizer!" Blair grabbed the black book, a look of joy on her face.

Drake had had a Filofax once. The executive size. He hadn't made a move without consulting it. The fact that she'd jumped overboard with hers told him she felt the same way he'd felt. But those days were over for him, thank God.

Shaking his head, he held out his hand to help Blair out of the dinghy.

A rip accompanied her climb from the boat. They both ignored it, though Drake noted the well-shaped leg it revealed, and walked over what was left of the wooden dock. Here and there, boards were missing. After a few feet, the walkway ended and they trudged through sand until they reached the golf-cart track.

"This is perfect," Blair said from behind him. "I have notes in here that will prove Armand—"

"Nobody in San Verde will care one way or the other what Armand did or didn't do." Drake held a low-hanging branch out of her way.

She ducked under it. "He left me floating in the Gulf of Mexico."

"You jumped."

"He's swindled people."

"They should have been more careful."

She spluttered. "He *lied* to me."

"*You* should have been more careful."

The golf-cart track intersected with the main drive of the lodge and continued in a loop that would bring it by the six cabanas on various parts of the tiny island. Three of the outer cabanas had been flattened. All had suffered damage. The nearest one to the lodge wasn't as bad as the rest and Drake had spent a week or so living in it until he'd made sufficient repairs to the lodge to be fairly certain the place wouldn't collapse on him. He'd get Blair some supplies and point her in the direction of the habitable cabana.

"He told me he was going to hold me prisoner for four months." Blair was still whining about Armand.

Drake wished she'd drop the subject. "I thought he was going to marry you."

"But it wouldn't have been a legal marriage and then he—" She broke off as they approached the dark hulk of the Pirate's Hideout Lodge. "What's that?"

"That," Drake said, "is my home."

3

"THAT'S NOT A HOME. That's a pile of driftwood."

"Isn't it great?" Drake gestured to the doorway, which was permanently open, since the door was propped beside it.

"What are you, a squatter?" Gingerly, Blair stepped over the rough boards and into the dark interior. Drake had disappeared inside. She heard rustlings and stayed near the doorway.

"No, I own the place. All of it." Drake struck a match and a kerosene lamp dimly illuminated the interior.

Directly in front of her was a desk and telephone switchboard, though she didn't see a telephone. Drake was standing immediately to the left, at a bar.

Bottles still lined two of the mirrored walls, but the third section was bare and only a jagged piece of the mirror remained.

He hung the lamp on a nail in a post, and struck another match.

"There's no electricity?"

"Nope." Drake lit two more lamps. "Not tonight."

Blair could almost see the whole place. Chairs and tables littered the room. "So there *can* be electricity."

"There's a generator out back, but it's a noisy thing. I run it when I need to."

"Can I convince you that you need to now?"

He shook his head. "If you need more light, I've got another lamp around here you can use. And maybe a flashlight or two."

"How about a telephone?" Blair asked, thinking of the switchboard.

"No telephone. Electricity wouldn't make a difference for that, anyway."

"How am I going to call the police?"

He shot her a frustrated look, his bearded face forbidding in the lamplight. "I have a shortwave radio you can use *tomorrow*."

The tone of his voice warned her not to press the point. Well, too bad. "But Armand will be gone by tomorrow!"

Drake vaulted over the bar and ducked behind it. "By now he's in Mexico."

"Yes. We were going to spend the night in Sonoma Villa. If they hurry, the police can still catch him."

When he stood, Drake was shaking his head. "You think he's going to sit around in Sonoma Villa and wait to be arrested?"

Actually, Blair did expect Armand to make some excuse to their guests—probably that she was seasick—and let them off in Sonoma Villa as scheduled. She smiled grimly. She'd upset his plans, but he was the type to recover quickly. "No, but the police in Sonoma Villa can be alerted."

"To what?" Drake shoved a canned drink

down the bar to her. "According to you, he hasn't done anything yet."

And he never intended to—that was the point. But when would Armand's inaction become a crime? Blair had no idea what he'd told the investors. Yet, surely there must be some law he'd broken. Unfortunately, until she could think of one, it appeared Drake had a point.

She needed time to organize her thoughts and think of possible courses of action. Obviously, if she couldn't convince this man of the urgency of her story, then what luck would she have with disinterested police in a tiny border town? They'd chalk up her story to the hysterical ravings of a woman in a wet wedding dress—as Drake was probably doing.

Blair eyed him as he took a long swallow from his drink. Time to drop the subject. She could deal with Armand's perfidy tomorrow.

Propping the life preserver against the wooden bar, she nodded to the can and asked him, "Have you got any diet drinks?"

Drake's mouth twisted in a mocking smile. "I think you can stand the calories this once."

She probably could. Anyway, her mouth had the most horrible taste. Blair sat on a bar stool and reached for the can. "It's cold!"

"Dry ice."

A cold drink. Suddenly nothing sounded better. From the first sip, Blair couldn't stop herself from guzzling the sweet liquid. It was all caffeine and sugar, but who cared?

"Hey, go easy on that." Drake's callused hand closed around her wrist.

"But I'm so thirsty," she complained. Her tongue seemed to swell in her mouth.

"See how your stomach handles this much." Sympathy flashed in the depths of his usually dispassionate gaze.

She closed her eyes as a sudden queasiness came over her, but it soon passed.

"How are you feeling now?" he asked when she opened her eyes to find him watching her.

"Hungry. I haven't eaten since breakfast."

"Let's see what we've got back here." Drake reached beneath the bar and brought out a box of crackers and spray cheese in a can.

"You're kidding."

He stared at her. "I like junk food. And if I want to eat junk food, I'll eat junk food. I eat plenty of fish. I grow vegetables. I pick fruit. My body can handle a little Jiffy Cheez." He ripped open the cracker box and mangled it in the process.

"I was only commenting." What a grouch. "It was unexpected, that's all."

Drake offered her a cracker. "I thought the crackers would settle your stomach."

"Thanks." She took one.

He held up the can.

In the interest of harmony, Blair nodded.

Shaking the can, Drake flipped off the top and squirted a perfect rosette onto her cracker.

She laughed. "You're good at that."

"Hours of practice."

"Just how many cans have you got back there?"

He squirted cheese on three more crackers. "I order it by the case."

"It's not bad," Blair admitted, though the cheese probably wouldn't have tasted so good if she hadn't been starving.

She studied Drake as she chewed. It was hard to tell how old he was. He wore a New York Knicks cap, and neither the scraggly locks of hair that hung beneath it nor his beard were streaked with gray. Squint lines around his eyes could be due to age or hours in the sun. He wore a knit shirt, which revealed tanned, muscled arms, cut-off jeans and holey deck shoes on his feet. Was he good-looking? Maybe, but the beachcomber look had never appealed to her.

No, you like suave, well-dressed fakes.

The thought sickened her. She and the others had been taken in by Armand largely because of the way he'd dressed and the lies he'd told. No one had looked beneath the surface.

What a snob she was. Here she was criticizing this poor man's appearance after he'd shared his Jiffy Cheez with her. She ought to be ashamed.

"Here you go," he said, pushing another cracker toward her.

A familiar form wiggled at her. "It's an elephant! How'd you do that?"

"Like this." With a few squirts, Drake fashioned an alligator.

"You're good." As she ate the elephant, Blair watched Drake sculpt a cat, a dog and a rhinoceros—or it could have been another elephant with a misshapen trunk. Blair doubted it, though. He was really quite skilled at cheese sculpture.

After eating half a dozen of Drake's cheese animals, she pronounced herself full.

"Better now?" he asked.

She nodded, feeling sleepy. Probably a delayed reaction setting in.

He came out from behind the bar. "Follow me, and we'll get you settled."

She slid off the bar stool. "What happened to this place?"

"Hurricanes. Three of them." He handed her a lamp. "Two early in the season and one at the tail end."

Blair accepted the lantern. She held on to her soggy planner.

"This place used to be a resort. This is the lodge." Drake gestured with his lamp. "We're passing through the lounge. Restaurant's through there. The kitchen, laundry, housekeeping and so on is this way." He swung the light to the left and indicated that she should turn.

"We're walking through the rec room."

Silently, careful of her bare feet, Blair followed Drake through the ruined lodge. At every turn, she expected to see signs of repairs in progress, but as far as she could determine, nothing had been done for quite some time.

The odor of mildew permeated the air. The night sky was visible through holes in the roof, and water had rotted several interior sections.

The only room that looked vaguely inhabitable was the rec room, and it appeared that this was where Drake slept.

It was a spacious room with Drake's bed against one wall. By shifting chairs around, Blair could have a little privacy. It wouldn't be the best accommodations, but she could stand it for one night.

"Come on." Drake gestured impatiently from a doorway at the end of the hall. "This is the linen closet. We've got sheets, towels and spare uniforms in here." He pulled the items off the shelves and piled them into her arms. "You want a medium or large T-shirt?"

"Medium."

He started to take a yellow one from the stack.

"Yellow isn't my color," Blair said. "Could I have one of the teal ones?" She pointed.

Drake looked as though he was about to say something, apparently thought better of it and replaced the yellow T-shirt. "Here you go." He set a teal square on the stack in her arms.

Looking down at it, Blair could see embroidered writing above the pocket. "Pirate's Hideout. That's what the sign said out front. Is that the name of this place?"

"Good guess." He piled something khaki over the shirt.

"You don't have to be sarcastic. I was just making conversation."

"You don't have to make conversation. In fact, I'd prefer it if you didn't." Drake positioned a small rattan basket on top of the stack. Inside were the usual hotel toiletries.

This was working out far better than she'd expected when she'd first seen the building.

"I nearly forgot." He stood on a metal shelf and reached for an unopened clear plastic bag containing an off-white fabric. "Mosquito netting. I'd

suggest you make hanging it your first priority."
He scooted it under the rattan basket.

The stack was so high, Blair had to hold the little basket in place with her chin.

"If you think of anything else you need, you
can poke around in here all you like. Food's in the
kitchen next door. There's a whole pantryful of
cans. Trouble is, the labels are gone."

"I bet that keeps your meals interesting."

"I've had some strange ones," he admitted, and
led her back the way they'd come.

When they came to the rec room, Blair started
to go inside.

"That's my room." Drake continued down the
hall.

Blair stopped. "I assumed…it's big enough for
both of us."

He turned around and stared back at her. Dark
eyes looked her up and down, then held her gaze.
"No." Pivoting abruptly, he continued down the
hall.

The incident unsettled her. She couldn't read
the look on Drake's face—probably because of his
beard. Beards didn't appeal to her. Come to think
of it, pencil-thin mustaches didn't appeal to her,
either.

Blair struggled to keep up as the bare concrete
floor scraped her feet. She could imagine what
this place must have been like. There had probably been carpet here once. The bar-area floor had
been a soothingly cool tile. She could picture lazy
afternoons spent sipping iced drinks as ceiling
fans circulated ocean breezes.

She wondered about Drake, living here all

alone. A hotel like this had probably been his dream and he'd run out of money to repair it. And without repairs, no guests would ever come. She remembered the season of storms two summers ago. The second hurricane wasn't so bad, but people had just finished or were still making repairs from the first one. Several areas of Houston had flooded, and there were stories of people with carpet installed only two weeks before it was all ruined again. By the third storm, the government had stepped in and refused to allow home owners to rebuild in certain areas.

That must be what had happened here. Too bad.

She expected Drake to show her to a room in another part of the lodge, but he headed out the front door. "Where are we going?" She found it difficult to negotiate the treacherous steps with an armload of linens and a kerosene lamp.

"Cabana number one," he replied.

Blair stopped. "Wait a minute—I'm not sleeping in the lodge?"

"No."

It was dark now and she couldn't see much beyond the circle of light made by her lamp. Drake's lamp was bobbing farther and farther into the mass of vegetation at the edge of the lodge's overgrown front yard.

Reluctantly, she plodded down the golf-cart track after him. The cracked asphalt was still warm from the day's sun, but it was hard on her feet. She couldn't wait to return to civilization.

She couldn't wait to get even with Armand.

Within a couple of minutes, just long enough to

walk out of sight of the main lodge, Blair saw Drake open the door to a small cabin.

When she stepped inside, she saw that he was carefully examining the walls and floor around the perimeter of the room.

"I don't see any scorpions, but check your shoes before—you don't have shoes. No problem."

"I happen to think it's a problem."

"Yeah, well, you can tie banana leaves or something on your feet." He held up the lantern and checked the roof.

Feeling the gritty coating of sand on the linoleum floor, Blair crossed the room and gingerly set her stack on the bare mattress of the bed. A low, square canopy frame stood guard over it.

"Looks like this place has stayed fairly waterproof." Drake lowered the lantern. "I lived here before I moved into the lodge."

Blair crossed her arms over her chest. "What's the point of making me sleep out here? Are you punishing me for the love-slave remark?"

"Punishing you? I fed you and gave you supplies. Then I took you out here and made sure there weren't any nasty old bugs to bother you. If you think that's punishment, then you've led a sheltered life."

"I don't want to stay out here by myself. If you don't want me sleeping in your precious rec room, then I'll sleep on the floor in the bar." She grabbed her stuff and knocked over the little rattan basket. Miniature bottles rolled everywhere. Muttering, Blair bent to pick them up.

"I don't want you in the bar, either."

"Why *not?*"

"Because I am not playing house for two weeks with a crazy woman. Hang the mosquito netting. Good night." He crossed to the door.

"Wait—what do you mean, two weeks?"

"That's when the next supply boat is due out. You can catch a ride into San Verde on it."

Blair grabbed at his shirt. "You can't possibly mean that I'm stuck here for two weeks!"

"That's exactly what I mean." He peeled her fingers off him.

"No."

"Yes."

"I can't spend two weeks here. You'll just have to take me to San Verde."

"I can't. The dinghy won't make the trip."

"You mean you're stranded here all the time?"

"Not all the time, but I am until I replace the carburetor in the launch."

"And when will that be?"

"In *two weeks* when the supply boat brings it!"

"Then you'll have to contact somebody to come and get me." Blair bit off each word. Honestly, eating all that Jiffy Cheez had affected his brain.

Drake rounded on her. "Let's get a few things straight, lady. I don't *have* to do anything. You can do whatever you want to this place to make yourself comfortable. I'll turn on the water pump so you'll have running water, but don't drink it. Either use purification tablets or drink bottled water. You'll find everything in the kitchen. You're going to have to catch your own fish and cook your own meals. But most important, you are to stay the hell away from me!" He jerked open the door. "And don't eat all the Jiffy Cheez!"

"I wouldn't dream of it!" Blair yelled after him and slammed the door.

The light wobbled as vibrations rattled the lantern.

She couldn't believe she was stuck here for two weeks. She would *not* be stuck here for two weeks. She would think of something.

And she wasn't going to stay alone in the cabana tonight, either.

Blair started to gather her things, then stopped. The sun had set and a high-pitched whine told her the mosquitoes were out. She was standing in a damp wedding dress in the middle of an island inhabited by a grumpy recluse. She was not in the best of negotiating positions.

Blair sank onto the mattress and wondered why she didn't feel like crying.

This was supposed to be her wedding night.

She thought of Armand—the Armand she'd seen in the waning light. The Armand who was who-knew-how-old. The Armand who'd planned to dump her, penniless—or pesoless—in a foreign country.

The Armand she could now admit that she'd never loved. She'd *wanted* to love him. She loved the whole idea of him and his family and generations of history. Was any of it true? Blair supposed she'd never know. She liked to think she would have made him a good wife and had looked forward to adding a few twigs to his family tree.

Now what? As she sat there, she slapped at a

mosquito, and decided to take Drake's advice about the netting.

Tomorrow she'd analyze her situation, organize her thoughts and plan what to do. All she needed was a plan. Fingering her agenda, she opened the rings and began spreading the damp pages on the floor to dry. The mosquito netting could wait.

Drake may have thought he'd won their encounter, but then he'd never come up against Blair when she had a plan. She'd get off this island, see if she wouldn't. She slapped at another mosquito.

Okay, maybe the mosquito netting *couldn't* wait.

4

THERE WAS A WOMAN on his island.

It was his waking thought.

Drake hadn't seen her this morning. Drake didn't want to see her this morning or any other morning. But in the event their paths should cross, he wrapped a towel around his waist after his swim and shower rather than enjoy the feel of the sun and salty breezes on his bare skin.

But that was as far as he was prepared to alter his routine just because there was a woman on his island.

Slicking back his damp hair, he strode from the outside shower, intended for guests to rinse off sand before entering the lodge, down the utility path to the generator, concealed behind artful landscaping entwined in metal fencing.

Drawing his hands to his waist, Drake glared at the generator in its bower of vegetation, thriving without any encouragement from him, then in the direction of cabana number one. He hated the sound of the generator. To him, it represented the pulsing vibrations of the city—something he'd come here to escape. Forever.

But *she* wanted electricity.

Since this was the emergency generator, there wouldn't be any power in the cabanas, but the ceiling fans and window units in the lodge should run.

The coffeemaker would work, too. Drake hadn't been able to convince himself he liked the percolated coffee he brewed on the propane stove. There was just something about coffee made from freshly ground beans and a drip coffeemaker.

Probably leftover from all those years he'd spent guzzling the stuff at the office.

The thought of his former life sent a tremor along his spine and reminded him of the letters that Mario had brought on his last supply run. Drake hadn't opened the letters. It wasn't necessary. They'd all be variations on the same theme, the when-are-you-getting-over-this-nonsense-and-coming-home song and dance.

He wasn't coming home. This *was* his home.

Inhaling the muggy air of his island, he closed his eyes, stepped from the shade into the sunlight and willed the warmth to ease the knots forming in his neck and shoulders. In the distance, the ebb and swell of the ocean as it rasped over the beach was far more tranquilizing than any commercially-prepared relaxation tape.

Drake stood there until an unknown insect crawled over his foot and broke the mood, much the same way the woman had disturbed his serenity. And as long as she was here, she was going to keep disturbing him, too.

He fueled the generator and turned it on, wincing as the roar drowned out the subtle sounds of his island paradise.

He shot another look toward cabana number one. He hoped she was happy now.

Feeling edgy, Drake headed for the kitchen, intending to reward himself with a decent cup of coffee. On the way, he detoured to the fruit trees rimming what had been the back lawn and patio. Peaches were ripe now. Lots of peaches. All at once. He was getting sick of eating peaches, but maybe what's-her-name—Blair—would eat some, he thought as he picked a few.

But this was the absolute final thing he was going to do for her. He'd saved her life and given her food, shelter and clothes. How much more was a man expected to do, anyway?

Drake shoved open the screen door to the kitchen, set the peaches on the counter and dug around for the coffee beans.

Once he had the coffee brewing, he stared at the peaches, grimaced and thought about eggs and toast. He could use the toaster now. If he had to suffer with the noise of the generator, then he might as well reap the benefits.

He was feeling almost charitable, when he turned to get a plate out of the cabinet at the exact instant Blair appeared in the doorway.

She looked as startled to see him as he was to see her.

Her wide-eyed gaze flicked over his bare chest, blinked at the towel, then returned to maintain a determined eye contact. "You obviously aren't expecting company, so I'll come back later."

Involuntarily, Drake tightened the knot on his towel, annoyed with himself for responding to her prissy expression.

Still, she hesitated in the doorway, casting a longing glance toward the coffeepot.

He knew that look. With a grudging "Help yourself," he got two mugs out along with his plate.

"Oh, *thank* you." Blair had filled the mug and brought it to her lips before he'd shut the cabinet door.

Drake tossed a chunk of butter in the skillet and covertly studied her. She seemed okay this morning, which was a relief because getting medical attention would be a major hassle. Her voice had a husky edge that probably had more to do with the time of day than swallowing saltwater. Yeah, she was okay.

She looked different dry. Her hair had fluffed out and lightened and the Pirate's Hideout uniform suited her, though it was hard to beat the see-through wedding dress.

He wouldn't think about that.

And he wouldn't think about the long tanned legs revealed by the khaki shorts, either.

The butter melting in the skillet bubbled. He turned down the flame and cracked the eggs. Real butter. Real eggs. Real coffee.

"You've got enough fat in there to clog the arteries of a third-world nation."

And a real pain. "I like fat."

She poked at the loaf of bread. "White bread?"

"Yes, *white* bread." The sneer in her voice got to him. "It makes the best bacon, lettuce and tomato sandwiches. You see, whole-wheat bread has a rough surface and holds too much mayo. White bread will give you a smooth foundation on which to build your masterpiece." He held up a piece and ran his fingers over the surface. "After the mayo, you slap on a quarter-inch slice of the sun-warmed beefsteak tomato you've just picked and—here's where people usually go wrong— then comes the lettuce. And not iceberg lettuce. People use iceberg and it's too hard. Gouges the bread."

"No iceberg," she repeated in a wary voice. She took a step backward.

"No, ma'am. What you want is bib lettuce. Soft. Makes a perfect bed for the bacon. Baby bib is superb." He brought his fingers to his lips and kissed them. "After that, you add your four pieces of bacon, another slice of tomato and top it with the bread." He popped the bread he held into the toaster. "Nothing better."

Blair looked dazed. "What were you—the chef here?"

"No."

"Bartender?"

"No." He turned back to his eggs. Couldn't she just be quiet and drink her coffee? Or better yet, leave?

"Obviously you weren't working in a capacity that required you to be nice to the tourists."

"Obviously." Drake tilted the skillet and spooned hot butter over the tops of the eggs.

Blair moved closer—after pouring herself another mug of coffee. At this rate, there wouldn't be any left for him. But she'd poured a mug for him, as well.

He acknowledged it with a nod.

"So…you were a hands-off kind of owner?"

"What?"

"I'm trying to find out what you did around this place." She eyed him speculatively over the rim of her mug.

"I didn't do anything. I bought the place after it closed."

"And it looked like this?"

"Pretty much."

"How long have you been here?"

"Since last fall."

"You mean, you've spent all this time here and…" Her eyes narrowed. "I don't believe you. You *are* a squatter. *That's* why you won't let me contact the police, isn't it? Because nobody knows you're here!"

He could strangle her and nobody would ever know. No wonder Armand had just sailed off into the sunset.

Drake drew a deep breath and spoke in a carefully controlled voice. "The police department in San Verde consists of Jorge, who also runs a vegetable market, and Mario, his nephew, who was deputized solely because he has a boat and can keep an eye on the marina. Jorge's wife, Lupe, is the dispatcher, if you will, because the police radio is right by the cash register. The market closes at sundown, so most likely nobody would have been around to hear you whine about Armand. If you ask me—"

"I *didn't* ask you!"

"Of course not. That would have been the smart thing to do!" Drake's voice was louder than he intended. "Lady, you ought to be thanking your lucky stars that I'm nothing scarier than a burned-out commodities trader, because you have no brains. Not one single...solitary...cell!"

She smirked. "I'm not the one who bought the world's largest pile of driftwood."

He'd ignore that. He wouldn't forget it—he'd just ignore it for now. "Let's say I am a criminal on the lam. You've stumbled onto my hiding place, but for some reason I'm feeling indulgent and I decide to let you live. Whatever you suspected, wouldn't the intelligent thing be to play along and let me think I'm fooling you until you can get off this island? After all, nobody knows you're here, do they?"

Her eyes widened.

"Yes, that's right. You're all alone. With me. And nobody knows." He leered.

"A-Armand—"

"Armand?" He shook his head. "Armand is history. He won't even bother to report you missing."

The flash of uncertainty in her eyes sparked unwilling sympathy in Drake. Even a little guilt. After all, she *had* been going to marry the guy. His betrayal must have hurt and Drake shouldn't have rubbed her nose in it, no matter how much she got on his nerves.

He wasn't fit company for humans—especially females, which was why he wanted her off his island. He had to get her off the island. Mario could be bribed—if he had something to bribe him with.

The toast popped up. They both looked at it. The sound of frying eggs filled the silence between them. She was subdued now, and when she sipped her coffee, Drake thought he saw her lip quiver. He groaned inwardly. Not the whipped-puppy look. Anything but the whipped-puppy look.

"Are you hungry?" he asked, guilt roughing the edge of his voice.

She swallowed. "Usually, I don't eat anything for breakfast but fruit and coffee—"

"Fresh peaches right over there," he interrupted.

"But today, for some reason, I'm ravenous." She gave him a tremulous smile. A brave little I'm-doing-the-best-I-can smile.

Nuts.

"Where do you keep the silverware?"

Breakfasting together would set a dangerous precedent—but it would be the last thing he'd do for her. After that, she was on her own. "In the drawer over there." He pointed.

She may have sneered at his eggs, but she gobbled them up fast enough. The white toast, too.

Drake cracked two more eggs into the skillet.

"Why haven't you fixed this place up?"

She should have seen it when he first got here. "It's livable."

"Barely." Blair got up from the table and, without asking, ground more beans for another pot of coffee. She was making a serious dent in his supplies and she considered it barely living?

"You have clothes, food, shelter and some of the prettiest scenery around," he said. "What more do you need?"

She stuck out a foot. "Shoes."

Would she never be satisfied? He sent her a long look. "Watch the eggs."

Grumbling to himself about ungrateful cast-aways, Drake stalked toward the utility room, grabbed a net bag filled with the rubber thongs Pirate's Hideout had thoughtfully provided for its guests, and dumped it at Blair's feet. "There. Shoes. Now you have everything."

But was she surprised? Grateful? No.

He rescued his eggs and ate them directly from the skillet.

He was tense, tense in a way he hadn't been for eight months. He had to get away from her—couldn't she tell?

No, she kept jabbering and trying on thongs.

"What did you say you were before you came here?"

He didn't want to answer. "Commodities futures trader."

"In…?"

"New York." Stomach roiling, he clipped the words. *Go away.*

"Ooh, Wall Street. Sounds exciting."

Drake swallowed. He could feel the food sitting in a lump in his stomach.

"When are you planning to go back?"

Memories flashed. Caffeine-fueled marathons, staring at numbers until they swam, the roller-coaster ride of fortunes won and lost, and adrenaline rush when he hit big—the nausea when he didn't…the relentless pressure, the expectations… "Never." He stared at the last of his eggs, stood abruptly and scraped them into the trash.

Blair seemed oblivious to his inner turmoil. "Hey, I found a pair that fits." She paced back and forth. "Thanks."

Drake mumbled and filled the sink with soapy water.

"What is that hideous racket?" she asked after gathering the rejected thongs into their net bag.

"The generator." Drake held out a faint hope that she'd beg him to turn off the noisy thing.

Blair perked up. "You mean we've got electricity now?"

"In places."

"What places?"

"The lodge, mainly, but don't go plugging stuff into any old outlet. I've got a power strip in the rec room."

"I don't have any stuff."

"You wanted to use the radio."

"I'm not allowed in the rec room," she reminded him.

"I'll make an exception this once." He left the dishes soaking in the sink—something he never did—and pushed past Blair.

He heard her follow him to the rec room, feet slapping in the thongs. With each slap, his irritation and the need to escape grew. "Here's the radio." He plugged it in and set it to the right frequency, hoping that Lupe was at the cash register this morning. Maybe Blair would have luck persuading another woman to help her get off the island.

"How do I work the radio?"

Drake seated her in a chair, noticing the scent of shampoo in her hair. It was the same stuff he used, but the scent seemed different on her. Sweeter. "Turn the knob." The radio crackled to life. "Press the microphone button when you talk and release it when you listen. That's all there is to it."

He stood, desperate to escape Blair and her sweet-scented hair. "I'm going fishing."

She gasped and started to get up. "I haven't had a chance to clean the boat."

Drake gently pushed her back in the chair. Her shoulder felt solid and soft at the same time. He let his fingers linger more than he should have. "I took care of the boat."

"You..." Blair glanced away then faced him squarely. "I think that's the nicest thing anybody has ever done for me." Her blue eyes were sincere. "I'm sorry I've been such a bother."

"No problem." What was he *saying*? She was nothing *but* a problem. One, big, irritating female problem. Drake backed away—away from the sincere blue eyes, the sweet shampooed hair and the long, tanned legs. Away from the brackets on either side of her mouth which she probably hated, yet gave her smile an attractive sophistication.

Away from the first woman he'd seen in eight months. "I'll be back. Late. Poke around all you like." *Run.* Run now.

"Drake?"

"What?"

"Wouldn't you like to get dressed first?"

THE FEEL OF HIS HANDS on her shoulders remained long after Drake collected his clothes and left. No matter how cranky he acted, there was caring in those hands.

He'd fed her, clothed her, sheltered her and

saved her life and she hadn't really given him much thought at all. Last night, she'd dismissed him as a reclusive, ill-tempered beachcomber. She hadn't even considered him as a man, but she hadn't considered any man as a man since the suave Armand had come into her life. Men as men had ceased to exist. They had become people.

Drake, the person, had rescued her yesterday, but once she'd encountered him in his towel at breakfast, she'd become aware of him as a man. She'd tried not to be, since he seemed so laid-back about his attire, but after all, it was *only* a towel, and a low-riding one, at that.

He was better-looking than she'd first thought and probably younger. She still wished he'd lose the beard, but with his hair slicked back, she could see the elegant shape of his head and forehead.

But who cared about an elegant forehead when faced with a broad, bronzed back, impressive chest and flat stomach? Maybe doctors should rethink their warnings about high-fat diets. Drake's body certainly hadn't been adversely affected.

And the horrible thing was, after seeing Drake with his smooth, golden torso, she was forced to admit that she'd avoided considering Armand as a man at all. Or rather, she had, but preferred not to.

She'd never even seen his torso. Never imagined it. She'd convinced herself that the physical aspect of their relationship was not important. Being comfortable together and fitting into his life *was* important.

Had she been insane?

Resting her hand on her chin, Blair stared out the rec-room windows to the dock, where Drake was loading a cooler and fishing paraphernalia into his boat.

He was still shirtless.

Blair sighed a little. She'd definitely been insane.

Not that being in her right mind now was going to do her any good, unless she got off this island in time to…to do something about Armand. The exact details would require some thought, but it looked as if she was going to have plenty of time to think of a plan.

Drake cast off and headed his dinghy out to sea, leaving her all alone just like every other man in her life—including Armand.

Drake had said he'd be back late. Blair would probably be gone by then. No matter what his opinion was, she knew the police would want to question her.

Tucking her hair behind her ears, she picked up the microphone. "Hello? I'd like to speak to the police, please."

Silence. She remembered to release the microphone button and there was still silence.

Maybe she needed to be more specific. "My name is Blair Thomason and I'd like to report a crime to the police in San Verde."

More silence.

She clicked the button. "Is anybody there? Hello?"

"Hello? Who's this?" asked an accented female voice.

Blair exhaled, unaware that she'd been holding her breath. She gripped the mike. "Blair Thomason. I'd like to report—"

"Where are you?"

That stopped her. "I don't know."

"Are you on a boat?"

"No. I'm on an island. There's water all around me."

"Sounds like an island, all right."

Blair wished she'd written a script so she could have sounded intelligent and calm instead of inane and scattered. "I'm on the Pirate's Hideout island."

"Ah, you're with Señor Drake, then. Let me talk to him."

"He's not—" She stopped and pressed the microphone button. "He's not here right now. He's fishing."

"Can you give him a message? Tell him the carburetor he wants isn't in stock and will have to be special-ordered."

Blair didn't care about any carburetors. "I need to report a crime—is this the police?"

"Yes, but hang on. I've got to ring up a customer."

Ring up a customer? When Blair had asked to report a crime? Weren't there rules about this sort of thing? Did the mayor of San Verde realize how lax the police department was?

Unfortunately, the silence gave Blair time to remember her last conversation with Armand. She had no doubt that she would look as guilty as he was, but she was counting on the fact that she'd jumped overboard to prove that she'd been a victim, not an accomplice.

"Okay, now, what was your problem?"

Collecting her thoughts, Blair told the woman about Armand's beef-shipping scam and how she'd jumped overboard when she'd discovered it. When she finished, there was silence. Too much silence.

"Hello?"

"You finally finished blabberin'? Lady, you gotta release that button once in a while. Listen, if this man is in Mexico—"

"But he's on his way to Argentina," Blair interrupted, forgetting that the woman wouldn't be able to hear her.

"—do anything."

She was going to assume the woman had just told her she couldn't do anything about Armand. "Can you alert the Mexican police then?"

"What for?"

Blair felt herself hyperventilating. "So they can catch him!"

"I don't know why they'd want him."

"To make him give back the money! My money!"

"Okay, okay. Do you know where he is?"

If Drake had let me call you last night, I would have. Maybe. "I believe he spent the night in Sonoma Villa."

"Okay. Is that it?"

"No! I think you should call the federal authorities, as well. American citizens are involved."

"That's a good idea. Let them take care of it. You finished now?"

"Aren't you going to send somebody to get me?"

"Sure. My nephew Mario takes mail and supplies there two times a month. You can ride in with him on his next trip."

Drake had said two weeks. "But I don't want to wait that long!"

"Well, lady, you're gonna have to. Mario'll be there about noon Wednesday after next."

"Ma'am, I can't stay on this island all that time. I'll pay your nephew or someone else to make the trip."

"What are you gonna pay with? You said this Armand took all your money."

Blair swallowed. "Credit card?"

The next sound she heard was laughter. From more than one person. Blair was obviously entertaining an audience. "Lady, we don't take credit cards."

If she'd still had her credit cards, Blair would have been more upset.

"Tell you what," the woman continued. "You want me to call your family or a friend for you?"

A friend or family.

Blair had plenty of acquaintances, but no friends. Certainly no one she could ask to get her out of this mess. As for family… "No," she answered shortly.

Something of her feelings must have come across in her last transmission.

"Hey, it's not so bad. Why are you in such a hurry to leave the island, anyway? Señor Drake is easy on the eyes, no? Eh, Rosa?" The mike cut off and the woman returned. "Rosa says you should forget this Armand. He's not comin' back." Blair heard murmurs of agreement in the background. "Señor Drake has been all alone for many months. A clever woman should be able to use that to her advantage."

5

BLAIR HAD NO INTENTION of seducing Drake.

She was going to get off this island. The San Verde police might not be interested in rescuing her, but Blair expected representatives from some branch of federal law enforcement to arrive within hours. Maybe they'd send a helicopter. She'd never flown in a helicopter before.

At the very least, the Coast Guard should be paying a visit.

Turning off the radio, Blair returned to the cabana. The pages of her agenda had dried and thankfully, the writing had remained surprisingly legible. Blair stuffed the bumpy pages back into their binder and folded her ruined wedding dress. Within half an hour, she'd stripped the bed, removed the mosquito netting and was on her way back to the lodge. Only at one point during the walk was the beach visible and though she searched, Blair didn't see any sign of Drake—or the Coast Guard.

Good, she'd have time to wash the dishes before she left.

Blair had time for that and a lot more. Once she started putting away the dishes, she realized the kitchen hadn't been organized with any thought to efficiency. Frequently-used items should be stored in the most accessible areas, but pots and pans had been placed clear across the kitchen, far from the stove.

From the kitchen, Blair could keep an eye on the beach and the back veranda. If she stepped outside, she could see around the corner to the dock. Still no sign of anyone.

With nothing else to do, Blair couldn't help herself. She switched the pots and pans to the cabinet near the stove and once she'd started, it was difficult to stop.

The contents of the drawers and cabinets needed cleaning, too. The humidity and salty air had left a film on the glasses, except for those few that Drake used regularly.

Blair washed them all, the entire time gazing out the window for any sign of an approaching boat.

Hours must have passed, though without a watch, she didn't know how many. It drove her crazy not knowing what time it was.

She got hungry and ate one of the peaches Drake had left on the counter. Then she ate the other one, feeling guilty. These were the best-tasting peaches she'd ever had in her life. In fact, they redefined her whole idea of what a peach should taste like. She hoped Drake wouldn't be angry that she hadn't left one for him.

The kitchen was in perfect order when Blair stepped outside to find nothing on the horizon. Maybe she should wait on the beach. What if her rescuers had missed her?

But a few minutes of relentless sun convinced Blair to turn back to the lodge. Waiting on the beach was a bad idea. She had no sunscreen and the short shadows told her that it was no later than midafternoon. Perhaps Drake had sunscreen, though his tan told her he foolishly didn't use it.

Blair entered Pirate's Hideout through the front, as she'd done last night. While she was waiting to be rescued, she'd snoop. After all, Drake had granted her salvage rights. Though she fully expected never to see him again once she left the island, she was curious—*mildly* curious—about a man who apparently had chucked his career to become a beach bum.

On a whim, Blair wandered through the ruined bar and dining room to the section of the lodge Drake hadn't shown her last night. The far side of glass walls had been broken. Someone had nailed plywood sheets over the openings, but had either given up, or another storm had ripped away the coverings. The side with the glorious view—the side facing the ocean—had borne the brunt of the storm and was now open to the elements.

And the elements hadn't treated this area kindly. Fine sand coated the black-and-white tiles, along with dead leaves and debris. Since no footprints marred the coating, Blair knew Drake didn't use this area.

She wished she had a flashlight as she passed the public rest rooms and found what must have been the hotel offices. The roof had caved in on this side and she hoped the manager's office was safe to enter, although she wasn't entirely certain about that.

Rusty file cabinets protected their mildewed

contents. Silt stains marked the walls where the room had flooded.

Watching for snakes, Blair amused herself by rescuing still-usable office supplies until she found a packet of brochures. The middle ones were practically untouched and gave Blair an excellent picture of how Pirate's Hideout had functioned in its heyday.

Words like *secluded, private* and *discreet* illustrated lush photographs of the stately lodge. Pirate's Hideout had been a retreat for the working rich. It was a place to find some privacy. To unwind and recharge.

Blair had never heard of it, but she wasn't among the working rich. One had to "apply" to be accepted as a guest.

There was a picture of a manicured lawn with rows of chaise lounges. For gentle amusement, the brochure invited guests to wander the nature trails and provided a map. Shuffleboard and croquet were offered as alternatives.

The brochure mentioned a library, which Blair hadn't seen yet, and showed the rec room with a pool table, piano and gaming tables.

The place screamed, in a genteel way, old-fashioned stateliness. Blair saw no television sets or anything about computers and faxes. The world was kept firmly at bay.

Pirate's Hideout had been prized for the very isolation that frustrated Blair now.

She also thought she understood Drake now. He was obviously bitter. No doubt he'd had dreams of restoring Pirate's Hideout to its former glory and had run out of money.

He, alone, had refused to abandon the island. He was fighting the odds—and losing.

Picturing Drake as a tragically romantic figure, Blair sighed and wandered back through the dining room. As she reached the bar, she remembered Drake and his cheese animals, which pretty much negated the tragically romantic aspects of his personality.

Actually, that cheese stuff hadn't been so bad. She could use a snack.

Walking behind the bar, Blair ducked below to search for the cheese and crackers and found a sign stuck over the box top.

"Off limits. This means you."

THE FISH WEREN'T BITING in the shady lagoon today, which suited Drake just fine. He wanted to be alone, though he'd definitely need to catch something soon with the way Blair was eating his supplies. Not that he minded particularly. When she was eating, she wasn't talking.

He hoped she'd convinced Lupe to send Mario out, but he doubted Blair had had any luck.

It was Mario's closely guarded secret that he got seasick. If Lupe knew, she pretended not to. Mario could stand the short jaunts around the San Verde Marina, but due to currents and land jetties, there was a stretch of rough water between Pirate's Hideout and San Verde that got him every time.

He was determined that no one would know. Anyway, once Drake got the hotel's launch running properly, Mario wouldn't have to make the trip anymore.

Drake spent the day fishing and napping and fishing a little more. By the time the shadows lengthened, he'd regained the serenity he'd sought by spending the day away from his unexpected refugee. Out of sight, out of mind.

He tossed back the two small fish he'd caught and nosed the dinghy toward the north side of the island to check the crab traps. He was in the mood for boiled crab to go with the last of the French bread that Mario had brought on his last supply run. Lots of melted butter…whatever looked good from the vegetable garden…and the time to savor it.

This was life as he wanted to live it. A life without deadlines and people constantly yammering at him. A life where he wasn't responsible for other people's fortunes. Life out of the pressure cooker.

Drake cut the dinghy's motor and drifted toward the traps, admiring the way the evening sun colored the sky and enjoying the fact that he could gaze for miles and miles and not see another human being.

Hauling the first trap out of the water, Drake plucked two good-size crabs from the basket and emptied the smaller ones and debris into the sea. He repeated the process with the other traps, tossing crabs into the bucket of water at his feet. As their white underbellies flashed, he was reminded of a certain wet white wedding dress and the woman who'd worn it.

The thought had come out of nowhere. One minute he'd been collecting crabs for his supper and the next moment he'd been thinking of *her*.

Was the image forever burned into his brain?

He felt his serenity melt away. He didn't want to think about her. Certainly not in that way. He didn't want to think of *any* woman in that way because he didn't want a relationship, and women always wanted relationships. A relationship was work and Drake was avoiding work. Therefore, he'd avoid *her*. It was the only way he'd survive the next two weeks.

There was no sign of Blair when Drake returned to the lodge. Carrying his bucket, he walked around to the kitchen entrance, stopping to pick a tomato. Looked as if there was going to be a bumper crop. He'd staggered the planting, but even so, maybe he could learn how to make ketchup or fresh Bloody Marys or something.

He entered the kitchen, set the crab bucket in one side of the double sink and reached under it for the stockpot. His hand knocked over a bottle of something. Dishwashing soap. He stared at various cleansers, sponges and a can of bug spray.

There was no sign of the pot.

He opened another cabinet, then another. "What the hell happened to my kitchen!" *Nothing* was where he'd left it.

"Oh, you're back." A nonchalant Blair appeared in the doorway.

"What did you do to my kitchen?" He jerked open drawers, slamming them shut again in frustration.

"I rearranged it to maximize efficiency." She looked pleased with herself.

"You what?"

"I simply put the objects you use most often within easy reach and grouped similar tools together." She sounded like a damn training video.

"I liked where everything was."

Shaking her head, Blair advanced into the room. "Once you become accustomed to this arrangement, you'll see how much more practical it is."

"But I don't know where anything is! What's practical about that?"

"It's arranged logically." She absently folded a tea towel. "If you use something several times a day, such as the cleansers, you'll find it close at hand. If an item is seasonal—"

"Seasonal?"

"Like Christmas decorations," she explained, ignoring his ill temper. "If an item isn't used very often, you'll find it in secondary storage."

Drake didn't have Christmas decorations. "What's secondary storage and what did you put there?"

"Secondary storage are those shelves and out-of-the-way nooks that aren't easy to get to."

"I don't have *nooks.*"

"Oh yes you do." She nodded her head.

Nooks shmooks. "I want my stuff put back the way it was." Drake was proud of the way his voice sounded, betraying nothing of the inner struggle he fought with himself to keep his hands from closing around her neck.

"No you don't. You're the type who is resistant to change, but once it's done for you, you'll like it."

Drake gritted his teeth. He'd been a teeth

grinder in his other life and had been forced to wear a plastic device at night. He hadn't worn it since he'd arrived at Pirate's Hideout. Something told him he shouldn't have thrown the thing away.

"Watch. I'll set the table." She walked to the cabinets next to the kitchen table and positioned herself. Without taking a step, she was able to gather plates, silverware and glasses and arrange them on the table.

"There. Easy, efficient and quick." She'd set the table for two, he noticed.

He glared at her. "Where is the stockpot?"

She smiled complacently. "In secondary storage. Such a large object—"

He smacked his fist on the counter. *"Get the stockpot!"*

Blair scrambled to the pantry, dragging a kitchen chair after her.

Drake willed himself to calm down and followed her. She was standing on the chair as she stretched to reach the top shelf where she'd put the pot.

The chair wobbled and Drake braced it. All he needed was for her to fall and break her leg. Then he'd have to wait on her. He'd never get any peace and quiet if she did something stupid like break her leg...her long tanned leg, which was now mere inches away.

Drake hadn't been this close to a female leg for many a moon. It didn't matter that this leg was attached to the world's most irritating woman. After months of countering the ill effects of years of stress to his body, his body was letting him know that certain parts of it wouldn't mind a little stress again. As though he needed the reminder, his mind replayed the image of Blair in her wet wedding dress. It was the only erotic image imprinted in his brain recently, which was why it frequently came to mind, he supposed. It couldn't have anything to do with Blair personally, because personally, she annoyed the hell out of him.

To distract himself, Drake tried recalling images from his past without success. They were gone. All gone.

Blair looked down at him with her big blue eyes. "Thanks, but the danger's past."

He had a horrible feeling that the danger was just ahead.

"Let me get the stockpot," he offered and straightened, careful to avoid looking at her legs.

"I got it up here. I can get it down." Blair reached again, worked the pot off the top shelf and handed it to him. Then she casually propped her hands on his shoulders and jumped down.

It was a good thing he was holding the stockpot, or he might have done something stupid, like putting his hands around her waist and pulling her close.

She probably would have slugged him.

"I'm sure there'll be other adjustments you'll want to make," Blair was saying as she dragged the chair past him. "Since I don't know your personal cooking-utensil preferences, I had to guess—"

"I don't want adjustments. I want everything put back exactly the way it was."

The look she gave him was patient, the smile

patronizing. "You're just saying that because you don't want to admit that you didn't arrange things in the best way."

He hadn't consciously arranged things at all. "No, I'm saying that because I don't know where anything is!" Drake punctuated his words by slamming the pot into the sink and turning the water on full blast.

She stalked over to the sink. "I can't believe you're being so stubborn. People pay me hundreds of dollars to organize their homes and businesses. It's what I do for a living. Naturally, I'd know more about ergonomics than you."

"But you don't know when to shut up." Drake turned off the water, carried the pot to the stove and lit the gas. It would be a few minutes before the water was boiling. Time for a snack.

Without another word to her, Drake left her in all her efficiently arranged glory and headed for the bar.

Flip-flops sounded behind him. "I organized the kitchen as a token of my appreciation. You can at least acknowledge the gesture, even if you intend to rearrange everything the instant I leave."

Drake stopped and stared back at her. "You're leaving? You found somebody to come out here and take you off my hands?" A broad smile creased his face.

Blair winced. "Not exactly."

"Bummer."

"As it stands, I'm still riding back on the next supply boat."

"Yeah, that's what I expected." He continued

to the bar, with Blair flip-flopping her way right beside him.

"Unfortunately, no law-enforcement agency is interested enough to get me off this island. I'm neither rich nor famous nor related to anybody who is."

She looked so incensed he refrained from saying *I told you so.* "What about Armand?" he asked instead.

"Until one of the investors files a complaint, the Securities and Exchange Commission won't act. Not enough time has passed to determine intent. So I told them *I* was filing a complaint, since he took my money, too."

She seemed to have covered all the bases. "Did you?"

"Yes, but when they heard we'd been engaged, they told me they didn't get involved in domestic disputes."

Drake rubbed the back of his head. "Maybe I can talk Mario into coming early if they get that carburetor in."

"Oh."

"Oh, what?" They'd reached the bar and Drake turned to face her.

"The lady on the radio said to tell you that they didn't have the part in stock and it would have to be special-ordered."

A delay? "No," Drake groaned, then mumbled a few choice words concerning the cruelty of fate. "You mean, I might be stuck with you even longer?"

"Unless you can figure out someone to bribe, yes."

"Don't *you* have anyone to bribe?"

"No—and if I did, I wouldn't have anything to bribe them with, remember?"

Drake groaned again.

Blair bristled. "It may interest you to know that I want to be here even less than you want me to be here!"

"I seriously doubt that," Drake snapped, then noticed the bar for the first time. "It looks different."

"I alphabetized the liquor bottles."

"For the love of Mike, will you just leave my stuff alone?" He vaulted over the bar and grabbed for the Jiffy Cheez, ready to consume an entire can.

It wasn't there.

Drake looked all over the bar but couldn't find the can. "Where in the hell is my Jiffy Cheez?" He glared at her.

She glared right back. "I've hidden it where you won't find it."

"*What?*"

Blair drew a deep breath. "Since it now appears that I'll be staying a while—"

"Give it back. Now." Drake felt a murderous anger well up inside him.

"No."

"No?"

Something must have shown in his expression, because Blair took a step back, even though the bar was between them. "If anything happens to me, I'll carry the location of your Jiffy Cheez to my grave."

Drake pounded the bar with his fist. "Why are you torturing me like this?"

"Because ever since you brought me here, you've been rude and inhospitable."

"Rude? Inhospitable? I saved your life! I gave you the run of the place." He glared at her. "Obviously a huge mistake on my part."

"You banished me to a shack in the jungle."

"For privacy!"

"Too much privacy. I can't stand the thought of wandering around here day after day all alone."

"And so I'm supposed to entertain you now, too? You want entertainment? Talk to Lupe on the radio."

Blair swallowed and glanced away. "I did. She won't answer anymore."

"Oh, great." He looked skyward. "You've alienated our only contact to the outside world."

"I didn't mean to!"

Drake leaned against the bar and regarded his newly alphabetized liquor supply. If he started at *A*—Amaretto—how long would it take him to get drunk? He wasn't normally a drinking man, so he had a feeling he wouldn't get much past *B*—bourbon. "So what's the ransom for the Jiffy Cheez?"

"I move into the lodge."

"Why?"

"I don't like being all alone out there. I had trouble sleeping last night."

Drake thought about it. He could always move out to the cabana if she proved too distracting. "You can't sleep in the rec room."

"Okay."

"And I'm not running the generator like I did today. I don't have enough fuel for that."

Blair nodded stiffly.

"Is that it?"

"No." She drew a deep breath. "I want you to behave civilly toward me."

He scowled. "I'm not a civil person anymore. That's why I'm living all alone on an island."

"But I'm not responsible for whatever drove you here and I shouldn't have to suffer for it."

Drake skipped *A* and grabbed the bourbon. He supposed she was right, but he didn't want to admit it. Besides, she was aggravating enough to sour the sweetest of dispositions. Look what she'd done to the garrulous Lupe.

"I don't want to follow you around all day or interfere with whatever it is that you do, but perhaps we could eat breakfast and dinner together and...talk."

"Talk about what?" Drake had been twisting the bottle cap and it finally came off. He sniffed. Smelled like bourbon all right.

Throwing up her hands in a gesture of apparent frustration, she paced in front of the bar. "About our lives. About philosophy. Politics. Religion."

"What's the point?"

"To get to know one another."

Where were the glasses? "I don't want to know you and I don't want you knowing me."

She met his eyes, then turned to gaze out the back of the dining area.

The setting sun washed the room in an apricot

light. It looked good on her. It would have looked even better if she hadn't stolen his Jiffy Cheez.

"I—I seem to have a talent for irritating people." She glanced at him.

"No kidding." Deliberately, Drake brought the bottle of bourbon to his lips and drank.

Liquid fire coated his mouth and throat. He gagged, but turned his back so Blair wouldn't see, and forced himself to swallow. Good God almighty, how could people drink this stuff?

"I don't know why I can't seem to make friends."

Drake would have told her if he'd been able to speak. Perhaps it was just as well that he couldn't.

"Except Armand," she added quickly. "Armand never lost his temper with me."

No, Armand was a swindler and a con man and he left you to drown in the Gulf of Mexico. Blinking his watering eyes, Drake saw her reflection in the cracked bar mirror. She'd wrapped her arms around herself.

"I know what he's doing is wrong, but I think, in his own way, he really liked me."

She continued to watch the sunset and Drake continued to watch her as the quiet poignancy of her words penetrated the wall he'd erected against the human race.

He'd only thought she was irritating to him—anyone would be while he was in his current state of mind—but he hadn't realized she affected everyone the same way. Or that she was aware of it.

Slowly, he returned the bourbon bottle to its place in the alphabet. He hadn't paid much attention to her, but he didn't think she'd mentioned someone wondering where she was or worrying about her. She'd been getting *married*. Weren't there bridesmaids or family or guests to notice that she was missing? And come to think of it, why should she have to depend on the police to rescue her? Wasn't there anyone else she could ask?

But Drake already knew that if there had been a single person Blair could have contacted, she would have. She was thorough that way. Instead, she was holding his Jiffy Cheez hostage in exchange for a little conversation.

He'd been a rotten, ill-tempered jerk.

But he didn't have to stay one.

He turned around and the movement drew her attention. "Blair," he said, deliberately using her name. "I've got a pot of boiling water and a bucket of crabs." He lifted a hinged section of the bar and walked under it. "Would you care to join me for dinner?"

She blinked at him suspiciously. "Are you sure?"

He nodded.

"Okay." Her smile lit up her face. It was a nice face, scrubbed free of makeup. "I'll get a can of Jiffy Cheez."

Drake reached for her hand and laced his fingers through hers, preventing her from pulling away.

When she looked at him in puzzlement, he smiled. He was out of practice, so it was a bit lopsided. "I don't need the Jiffy Cheez."

6

"DID YOU FIND the library while you were exploring?" Drake asked after they'd put away the last of the dishes.

"No," Blair answered, remembering that the brochure mentioned a library. "I'd like to see it, though."

"Then follow me." He hung up the dish towels, handed her a lantern, then led the way to the rec room.

During dinner, he'd been a pleasant companion—not exactly charming—but he barely resembled the grouch he'd been ever since she'd arrived. He hadn't talked much, but he *had* talked. She might have been fooled into thinking he hadn't minded her company, but she wasn't that gullible.

Blair was amazed to discover that he hadn't read a newspaper or magazine in eight months, and only seldom listened to the shortwave radio. She started to fill him in on recent current events, but he cut her off with a curt, "If I were interested, I would have listened to the radio."

She wanted to ask him what he was doing here, living away from everyone and everything, but knew he wasn't ready to tell her. Not that he'd ever be. She was a temporary interloper, only a few cans of Jiffy Cheez away from being ignored once again.

At least he'd stopped complaining about her arrangement of the kitchen. As they washed and dried the dishes, he watched without comment where she put everything, and though he stopped short of complimenting her, Blair got the impression that he wouldn't be rearranging things after she left.

Following him down the hallway, Blair admitted to herself that she was intrigued by Drake. She wouldn't go so far as to call it a full-fledged attraction, but now and then he showed her another glimpse of his personality—a personality that was far more appealing than that of the curmudgeonly beachcomber he portrayed.

When they reached the rec room, Drake pointed to a double door that Blair hadn't noticed before. It was painted the same celery color as the walls and the wainscoting continued uninterrupted, but when Drake drew it open, Blair stepped into another world.

"This room wasn't damaged at all," she said, noting the lush Oriental carpet covering the tile. Three of the walls were lined floor to ceiling with books. Small writing desks dotted the room, along with overstuffed chairs and side tables. The last wall was made up of French doors opening onto an enclosed patio.

"These windows were boarded up during the storms, but water did blow in through the cracks." He gestured to a far corner near the ceiling. "The roof leaked in that area. Rain dripped behind the shelves and warped them."

She searched for water stains and didn't find any. "Everything looks fine now."

"That's because I repaired the roof and rebuilt the shelves. I didn't want the books to be damaged any more than they had been." He walked to the shelves and ran his hand over the volumes in a revealing caress. "Some of the bindings are water-spotted, but I think that adds character."

His smile invited her to agree and she nodded, struck by the change in him. His movements were slower and more relaxed and he was no longer engaging her in verbal skirmishes. Obviously, this room was a demilitarized zone. "You spend a lot a time in here, don't you?"

"Every evening." He set his lantern on one of the reading tables and moved around the room lighting wall sconces and other lanterns. "I'm working my way through the classics by candle-light."

"Sounds like a program on public television."

He laughed and Blair realized it was the first time she'd heard him genuinely laugh because he was amused and not because he was mocking her. "My mother would tell me I'm ruining my eyes, but I get a pretty good light."

Her mother wouldn't have noticed whether Blair was reading or not. Actually, Blair had been a heavy reader. She and her mother had moved frequently and the library had been her one constant from city to city.

The room was silent except for a faint buzz from the lanterns and the tapping from bugs hurling themselves against the glass. Drake had turned off the generator before they'd eaten and

Blair enjoyed the silence. She was beginning to think like Drake—electricity just wasn't worth the noise.

"What are you reading now?" she asked, trying to see the title on the end table next to a cushy leather club chair. She guessed this was where Drake read each night.

He grinned. "Anne Rice. I intend to read all the Shakespeare plays, but I need a break every now and then."

"From Anne Rice, or Shakespeare?"

He laughed again. "Both."

Blair wandered over to the shelves. "What will you do when you've read all the books?"

Drake pulled the gauzy drapes and gazed around the room. "I've got years of reading in here. You know how many people say they want to read *War and Peace?*" He tapped his chest. "I have. I didn't like it, but I read it."

"I hope I'm not here long enough to read *War and Peace.*" When he didn't respond, she glanced at him. "That's okay. I know you hope I'm not here long enough to read *War and Peace*, either."

"Depends on how fast you read."

Not fast enough. She scanned the shelves thinking about all the hours she'd spent reading as a child. Somehow, she'd fallen out of the habit. "Do you have something lighter?"

"Such as?"

Blair shrugged. "I don't know—mysteries?"

Drake crooked his finger. "Agatha Christie? Or—" he hefted a fat book "—here's the complete Sherlock Holmes. And don't forget the ever-popular island reading, *Robinson Crusoe.*"

"I'll pass." Blair chose Agatha Christie and settled on the leather sofa, tucking her legs beneath her. Soon she forgot all about being stranded on the island and thwarting Armand.

Every once in a while, she looked over at Drake, engrossed in his own book, his long fingers carefully turning the pages. He was content and, for the moment, Blair was content, too.

Some time later, she roused enough to feel something soft whispering over her and being tucked around her shoulders. Then she burrowed into the sofa and went back to sleep.

DRAKE STARED DOWN at the sleeping woman, feeling a curious admiration. She wasn't so bad, he conceded. She'd actually gone hours without saying a word. He hadn't thought she was capable of it.

The room had that effect on a person—at least a person with any depth.

So Blair had depth. Who'd have thought it? He wondered what her story was, and not the Armand part, either. Maybe tomorrow he'd find out.

Drake extinguished the sconces and lanterns, one by one. When he reached the lantern next to Blair, he hesitated, then turned down the wick on that one, as well.

He'd leave the doors open in case she awakened during the night.

Climbing into his bed, Drake's last conscious thought was of Blair in that damn wedding dress.

BLAIR PEELED HERSELF off the leather sofa the next morning when a beam of sunlight caught her across the face.

Drake wasn't in the room.

Great. She'd fallen asleep. What if she'd snored?

After folding the white fleece blanket with the royal blue Pirate's Hideout logo embroidered on it, she checked her wrist, unable to break herself of the habit of looking at her watch.

No matter, it was breakfast time.

Blair peered into the rec room. Drake was already up and gone so she headed for the kitchen.

It was a bright morning that promised to become a hot day. Blair measured coffee beans into the grinder and pressed the button.

Nothing happened and several moments passed before she remembered that there was no electricity. Now she'd have to use the canned ground coffee and figure out how to use that old stove-top percolator she'd seen yesterday.

Blair was watching the water bubble, wondering if she was going to manage to make drinkable coffee at all, when a shadow crossed the doorway. Drake stepped over the threshold, caught sight of her and tightened the knot of his towel.

"Wearing your usual morning attire, I see," Blair said, dragging her eyes away from his golden torso.

"Usually I don't bother with the towel," he said, approaching the coffeepot. "You could say I'm being civilized."

Blair felt herself blush. That's right. She owed him Jiffy Cheez.

He leaned against the counter and watched her, too closely for her peace of mind.

"I'm fishing today. You want to come?"

The invitation caught her completely off guard. "I—really? That's not part of the deal."

"Forget the deal. You want to fish with me, or not?"

Uppermost in her mind was trying to figure out why he'd asked her. "Well, I...why?"

"We need food, for one thing. For another, I now know it's possible for you to keep your mouth shut." He opened a drawer. "Hot pads?"

Blair pointed to the next drawer over.

"Coffee's done." Drake pulled the pot off the burner. "So, are you fishing with me, or not?"

Blair was cautiously pleased with Drake's invitation, but she didn't want to take advantage of him in a moment of weakness. "I had planned to try and mend fences with Lupe and see if she'd had any luck finding a way to get me off the island," she offered, waiting for his reaction.

"Fine. Suit yourself." He'd grabbed a mug, but forgot to use the hot pad when he reached for the coffeepot. When he jerked, coffee sloshed out of the pot. Drake drew in a sharp breath between his teeth.

Blair ran cool water and pulled his hand under the stream. They stood there for several seconds.

"You don't have to stand here and hold my hand."

Blair stepped back. "Do you think Lupe will speak to me today?"

"I have no idea."

"I probably ought to try and contact her, don't you think?"

"Fine. I said *fine*." He flung an arm in the direction of the rec room. "Stay here or fish. I don't care."

Blair hesitated. "I don't know how to fish."

"Everybody knows how to fish."

"Well, I don't."

He'd been staring at his hand. Now he stared at her.

"Would you teach me?" she asked.

"Nothing much to teach."

"I'm sure there're all kinds of techni—"

"You put a hook in the water! The fish either bite or they don't!" He glared at her, then at his hand again.

"Does your hand hurt?"

"Yes, my hand hurts!"

"Sorry. I was just trying to help."

"If you want to help, pack us a lunch." Drake turned off the water. As he dried his hand, her silence must have registered. "What?"

"You're sure you don't mind me coming with you?"

His gaze swept over her. "I wouldn't have asked you if I minded."

She could tell he'd made an effort to keep his annoyance in check. A pleased smile touched her lips. "Then it's a date."

A wary look crept into his eyes. "Hey, this isn't a *date* date or anything."

"Well, technically—"

"Technically nothing."

Blair went directly to the coolers she'd packed

away. "You issued an invitation and I accepted. I'd call that a date."

"This isn't a date!"

Blair was enjoying herself. "Then what would you call it?"

"I'd call it fishing, because that's what it is. We're going to catch some fish and then we're going to clean the fish and then we're going to cook the fish, because otherwise, we're going to run out of food!"

"Clean the fish?" Blair made a face as she scrounged for something to pack for lunch. The bread was nearly gone. "That involves knives and fish guts, doesn't it?"

"Yeah, and then we take the heads and put them in the crab traps." From the way his eyes crinkled at her over his coffee mug, she thought he might be smiling. A good sign.

"Oh, joy." She straightened. "Looks like it's peanut butter and jelly for lunch."

"Sounds okay." He rinsed the mug and set it in the sink. "Come on down to the boat when you're ready."

"You've never been fishing before? *Never*?"

Blair shook her head. "I told you I didn't know how."

Drake pulled his cap low over his forehead and squinted at her. "Your daddy never took his little girl fishing?"

"Not this little girl." She gazed back at him musingly. "I don't think he's the fishing sort."

Drake noticed she spoke in the present tense. He'd wondered, not that he wanted to, but it had

begun to nag at him that she could disappear the
way she had and nobody seemed to care one way
or the other. Armand had his reasons for keeping
quiet, but wasn't there anybody else who would
be interested in knowing that she hadn't gotten
married as planned?

Drake cut the dinghy's motor and they drifted
into the shady lagoon where he did his best fishing. "Were you eloping?"

She'd been dragging her hand in the water.
"Where did that question come from?"

"You talk about your dad as though he's still
alive."

"Yes, why wouldn't he be?"

"He wasn't at your wedding?"

Blair laughed. "He and my mom split up when
I was little. He surfaces every once in a while and
offers to take me to lunch. Then he stands me up.
I'm not even sure where he is right now."

"Your mother then." Drake handed her a fishing pole. "Wasn't she there?"

"Mother has been married so many times, herself, that weddings have lost their appeal."

So they weren't a tight-knit family. That wasn't
necessarily a bad thing, Drake decided, thinking
of his own interfering mother. "But this was *your*
wedding. Or have you been married before?"

Eyeing the fishing pole, she shook her head.
"How do I get the hook loose?"

Drake showed her how to work the simple reel,
but he wasn't ready to drop the subject. "You said
there were guests on the boat."

Her glance told him she didn't want to discuss
it. "Armand's friends. Where are the worms?"

"We're using canned corn," he explained impatiently. "Didn't you—"

"I may not have been fishing before, but even *I* know you're supposed to use worms," she insisted.

"It's too much trouble to dig them up. Didn't any of *your* friends—"

"Well, how am I supposed to get corn on a hook?"

"Forget the hook!"

She blinked at him, her jaw set stubbornly.

He snatched the pole from her and shoved a few kernels of corn on the hook. "There. Cast it in and—not like that!" He ducked as the hook flew inches from his arm. "You'll catch the hook on me."

It plopped into the water. "But I didn't."

"Just remember for next time. Now, about your wedding…"

"I *don't* want to discuss my wedding." She gazed determinedly out at the lagoon.

"Why weren't any of *your* friends and family there?"

She had hunched over, her elbows resting on her knees. As he watched, she tucked a lock of brown hair behind one ear.

A tiny gleam drew his eyes to her earlobe where a chaste gold-ball earring shone. It was the only adornment she wore.

She didn't need adorning to look good. Her skin was the kind that tanned easily and the few freckles sprinkled across her nose contributed to her natural outdoorsy look. Some women could carry off the casual look and some couldn't. Blair could.

"It was just going to be a civil ceremony," she said with a sigh. "When we got to Argentina, we were going to be married in the de Moura family chapel where generations of de Moura brides have been married." There was still a remnant of anticipation in her voice. "Armand has a large family and they all live on..." She trailed off with an embarrassed glance at him. "I suppose that's all a lie, too." Swallowing heavily, she turned away. When the hair fell from behind her ear, she didn't push it back.

"Armand is a jerk." Drake wanted her to believe that with an intensity that caught him unaware.

She lifted her shoulder in a small shrug. "I was stupid. Stupid to think anybody—" She interrupted herself with a shaky breath. "I was just stupid, that's all."

Drake had spent most of his adult life working with numbers. In commodities futures trading, there wasn't time for emotion. There wasn't room for emotion. His clients exhibited one of two emotions: elation or despair, according to the reckoning at the end of the trading day. Nothing in between.

Whether or not slowing the pace of his life was responsible for a heightened awareness of the feelings of others, Drake didn't know. He hadn't been around others, except for Mario, since he'd come to the island. But Blair was here now and he found himself sensing her feelings. That she'd been hurt was obvious. What Drake thought was more significant was her acceptance of the hurt. She got a little quiet, sure, but mostly she brushed it away.

She'd had practice, he realized with a new certainty. She'd been hurt before—so many times she expected to be hurt.

"Hey, it could have happened to anybody," he said, and awkwardly patted her shoulder. The gesture felt awkward because Drake wasn't used to comforting by touch and because he wasn't sure touching her would be a good thing for either of them.

She stiffened at first, then relaxed when he didn't pull away.

Drake moved his hand in slow circles, then rubbed the muscles in her back. He could feel them beneath the teal knit Pirate's Hideout shirt. Though he and Blair were in dappled shade, her shirt was warm. He was warm. He bet she was warm, too.

If he'd been by himself, he would have stripped off his shirt and not given it another thought.

It didn't seem fair that he could take off his shirt and Blair couldn't.

Of course, she could if she wanted to. *He* wouldn't mind. And her lacy bra would cover anything important. He wondered if it would be as transparent dry as it had been when it was beneath the wet wedd— He gave her shoulder one last pat and eased his hand away.

"Thanks," she said. "I'm okay."

He hated that tone in her voice. "No, you're not okay! Damn it, Blair, you've got two living parents and you can't call them for help?"

"Oh, I see." She straightened and glared at him. "You want me off your island." She inched away from him.

"No." He reached for her arm, feeling the need to touch her again. "Well, yes, but I didn't mean it like that. I'm curious to know why you didn't call them. If you'd asked Lupe to call your mother, she would have."

She gave him a look he couldn't read. "Mother would tell me to wait for the supply boat."

Before he could question her further, a movement in the water drew their attention. Blair's float bobbed and disappeared beneath the surface.

"Pull up!"

"What?"

"You've got a fish!"

"I do?"

Drake grabbed for her fishing pole and jerked it up. "Start reeling it in."

Giving the task far more concentration than it deserved, Blair worked the reel. "It's heavy. The fish must be huge."

She looked so pleased with herself, Drake watched her instead of the float.

Blair finally wrestled the fish out of the water, squealed and laughed, letting it swing until Drake caught it.

"I thought it would be bigger."

"It's at least a pound and a half. A keeper." He removed the hook and tossed the fish in the bucket of water he'd brought for that purpose.

"What kind is it?"

"I don't know—a little ocean perch, maybe. I don't introduce myself, I just eat them."

Blair laughed, her eyes now shadow free.

As he gazed into her upturned face, with the freckled nose and the blond-tipped eyelashes, Drake wished he could have just three minutes alone with Armand-the-sleaze-bucket.

And Blair's parents, too.

"THIS WAS the hotel's boat? I didn't even know there was a boathouse." "Boathouse" might be a generous description for the open-sided ruin she saw, but Blair could see that Drake, or someone, had been making repairs.

"Yes, the *Pirate's Lady*. It's visible from the dock, if you know to look for it," Drake said. He tossed the rope over the pole, climbed out of the dinghy and helped Blair.

After they'd caught enough fish, Drake had taken her the long way back around the tiny island. The coast had been cleverly landscaped with inlets and sheltered coves where hotel guests could swim or play in paddleboats. Debris now littered the white sand, but Blair could see how appealing the coastline once must have been. Actually, it was still appealing.

Now, as she climbed out of the dinghy, Blair guessed that this dock had been where the guests landed. A wide asphalt path led the way up a gentle incline. "That's where the golf-cart track leads, doesn't it?"

Drake nodded. "If you follow the main road, you'll get to the lodge." He walked over to the dry-docked *Pirate's Lady* and stood, hands on his hips. "She was banged up pretty good, but I thought I could fix her."

"Are you a good mechanic?"

Drake grinned. "I'm a terrible mechanic. Every time I get this thing running, something else goes wrong."

"So you are stranded a lot."

"More than I intended to be, that's for sure. Someday, after I teach myself enough about it, I'm going to take off in this boat." He looked back at her. "I was going to work on her this afternoon. If you stick around, I'll find something for you to do."

He was being so decent to her, Blair thought she'd reward him by leaving him in peace. "Tell you what. I'll take the fish back to the lodge and fix a fabulous dinner for you."

His face creased into a pleased smile. "What are we having?"

"Well, fish."

"Of course."

"And I thought I'd raid the cans."

"Ah. Chef's surprise. I'll look forward to it."

Blair stepped back into the dinghy and retrieved the bucket of fish. "Okay, it's a date then."

"A date?"

She met his eyes squarely. "Yes, a date."

"A *date* date?"

"A dinner date."

They looked at each other, the silence broken only by the water lapping against the dinghy, and some noisy bugs.

"Okay. A date." Slowly, a smile spread across Drake's face. "I'll bring the wine."

7

BLAIR HAD NEVER CLEANED a fish before and hoped she never had to do it again. Fortunately, the professional cookbooks she'd found gave explicit instructions. Normally, Blair appreciated explicit instructions. Normally, she wasn't cleaning fish.

She saved the fish heads for Drake's crab traps, wrapped the fillets and set them in the ice chest.

Baking a peach pie was infinitely more pleasant. Although the flour she found was of indeterminate age, it was in an airtight canister and appeared to be okay. The peach trees were loaded with fruit. If Drake were smart, he'd can some. She hadn't found any canning jars and made a note to suggest that he order some.

Deciphering the contents of the cans in the pantry was actually kind of fun. By shaking them, she guessed which ones held the same things and grouped them together. They were all a fairly large restaurant size, so once she opened one, they'd be committed to eating what it contained for several meals.

She wasn't ready for a long-term commitment so she headed to Drake's kitchen garden.

The plants were more or less in straight rows and the garden could stand a little weeding, she thought critically. Then she proceeded to do so. Only after she was hot and sweaty did she think about a change of clothing. She could probably scrounge another shirt and shorts from the linen-storage room, but she had a horrible feeling she was going to play hostess to Drake without wearing any underwear.

A DATE.

He shouldn't have encouraged her, but nobody likes to be shot down.

Drake put away the last of his tools and wiped his face with his shirt. Blair probably meant she was getting out a tablecloth and candles, so he should spruce up a little. He could do that.

A date. When was the last time he'd gone out on a date? Long before coming to Pirate's Hideout, that's for sure.

The last time had been with Pamela and then it was only to keep his mother quiet. But afterward, she'd grilled him and he knew that if he hadn't asked Pamela out a second time, his mother would trot out some other candidate for her future daughter-in-law.

So he'd asked Pamela out again. And maybe a third time. He couldn't remember actually asking her, but he'd attended some charity dinner with her.

Then there were a few times when he took his mother to one of her functions and Pamela always seemed to show up. Between the "Pamela's going, too. Why don't we all go together in one car?" times and the "Look who's on my commit-tee!" times, it seemed he couldn't turn around without running into Pamela. He was careful not to encourage her, but then, she appeared to need no encouragement.

Drake neither liked nor disliked Pamela. She was one of those women who slyly watched, then molded herself to her surroundings. Pamela would always fit in. He just didn't want her fitting in with him.

Blair wasn't Pamela. He didn't even think they'd like each other very much. Pamela didn't irritate him the way Blair did. And Pamela wouldn't have decided to take a swim just before her wedding, either.

God, that took guts. Smiling to himself, Drake walked to the lodge, remembering that he'd promised Blair a bottle of wine.

SHE HAD NO IDEA what time it was or when Drake would be back. Blair wouldn't cook the fish until she knew he was ready to eat, but in the meantime, she'd prepared a salad and assembled a ratatouille of baby vegetables.

A lovely white tablecloth covered an unfortunately water-stained table, and Blair had selected the best two chairs from the pile of ruined furniture in the restaurant dining room. The upholstery was rotted, so she covered the seats with large dinner napkins and stapled the fabric in place.

She found about a million votive candles and liberally placed them around the room. Because the room was open and there was an ocean breeze in the evening, she wasn't sure how many candles would stay lit, but the more she had out the better her chances. The room looked great.

Blair, herself, was another matter.

She'd managed to find some white pants, probably part of a waiter uniform, that were a wee bit snug, and a white, buttoned shirt that was too big. She tied the tails under her rib cage and rolled up the sleeves. If she remembered to hold in her stomach, the pants looked just fine.

Her underwear was drying on a hook in the storeroom.

Oh, well, she thought, examining her reflection in the bar mirror. No visible panty lines.

Checking to make certain Drake wasn't around, Blair went to the hotel offices and pried open the rusty file cabinet where she'd hidden half the Jiffy Cheez. At least she knew Drake would like the hors d'oeuvres.

IT'S ONLY A stupid dinner, Drake told himself.

So why was he standing in front of a bathroom mirror with a razor in his hand? He hadn't shaved for months, but, hey, the weather was getting hot and he'd been meaning to shave off the beard anyway.

Once his beard was gone, Drake decided his hair was pretty shaggy. When he didn't wear his Knicks cap, his hair got in his face, so he'd just trim it a bit.

Okay, so he hacked off his ponytail. It got the job done and felt cooler, too.

He dressed in loose cotton drawstring pants and a matching overshirt he'd bought during the short time he'd spent in San Verde buying supplies, but not even for a date with Blair was he putting on hard-soled shoes. And the deck shoes were out of the question, so he decided not to wear shoes at all.

He stepped back and tried to see himself. "Not bad, O'Keefe," he murmured and grabbed the wine.

The wine collection had been one of the few pleasant surprises he'd come across during his stay here. The former owners had literally sailed away and never returned after that last hurricane. They'd given up and left everything behind.

Naturally, without electricity, the cellar wasn't kept at an optimum temperature and Drake was no wine connoisseur, but the few bottles he'd sampled had tasted okay.

This white one should be more than okay according to the prices on the laminated wine list.

He wondered if Blair knew wines. They could sample some and compare, he was thinking as he opened the kitchen door.

The kitchen was empty and the table wasn't set.

There was no sign of Blair.

Drake felt a prickle of alarm just before the heavenly smells of baking registered. He let out a breath. She was around here somewhere then.

Still carrying the wine, he walked the length of the lodge to the bar.

And then he saw her, sitting at a table, surrounded by papers, the glow of candles casting interesting shadows on her face.

She hadn't heard him approach and continued

to write in her agenda, concentrating on who knew what.

The more he was around her the better she looked. He was going to have to be careful. She was vulnerable, no matter what kind of front she put up.

EVERYTHING WAS READY except the fish. Blair even tried sculpting a few Jiffy Cheez animals, then gave up. Drake made it look easy.

She was hungry. Hungry and bored and tired of waiting for Drake to finish fooling around with his boat.

She'd been stupid to place any importance on this dinner. He obviously hadn't.

And why should he? They were just marking time until she left. She should remember that—she'd had plenty of practice in her life.

Blair was always leaving. She'd learned not to make close friends because it hurt too much to leave them behind. Her mother moved from place to place looking for something Blair could never figure out. Even as an adult, she couldn't figure it out.

Sometimes Blair felt like a dandelion seed pod, drifting on breezes until she could finally land and set root.

But where would she drift now? She had no job, no friends, no home and no money.

On that depressing thought, she wandered over to the windows and gazed out at the ocean. The sun hung low in the sky and the whole view looked like something from a travel brochure.

There was a soothing sameness to the gulf's ebb

and flow. People would pay—and had at one time—big bucks to have a view like this. It was a shame to let the lodge crumble. Rebuilding would be a huge task and, due to the island's remoteness, probably wildly expensive.

But it could be done with careful planning.

Detailed, methodical planning—the kind at which Blair excelled. She could do it, she knew she could. If Drake didn't want to bother, then Blair could be his agent. She *wanted* to be his agent. It would give her a job and a focus. Something she could do until she knew where to go next.

And if Drake needed money, he could take on a partner. Blair could help him there, too. If she'd learned anything from hanging around Armand, it was how to describe dreams in terms of profit-making potential.

The more Blair thought about it, the more enthusiastic she became. With the brochure to guide her, she smoothed her bumpy agenda-project sheets and proceeded to plan the resurrection of Pirate's Hideout.

She'd outlined a basic stage-one repair before she had to light the candles and then went right back to work.

"Good evening, Blair."

The deep voice startled her. She hadn't even heard Drake approach. Blair looked up, but the words of greeting died on her lips.

A stranger stood in the shadows by the bar.

She jumped to her feet, ready to run, when he stepped into the candlelight and she recognized him.

Drake. But a Drake she'd never imagined.

The loose, natural-colored clothes he wore glowed in the subdued light, imparting a cinematic heroic quality to his appearance. His hair was brushed back and the blond sunstreaks gleamed. He looked larger than life. He looked like something from her dreams. He looked nothing like Armand.

"You shaved."

Reflexively, he rubbed a hand over his jaw. "The beard was getting hot now that it's getting warmer."

With the beard gone, Blair saw that Drake had a strong, well-defined jaw and a well-shaped mouth.

Put it all together and he was handsome. Incredibly handsome. The kind of handsome that exists on a plane not inhabited by ordinary-looking people like Blair.

The kind of handsome that would never give her a second look—unless she was the only female on a deserted island, which she was.

Blair wanted to shrivel in embarrassment. She'd called this a date. How…presumptuous of her. Men such as Drake didn't date the ordinary.

And here she was in ill-fitting clothes, her hair all kinky and her face not covered in a speck of makeup.

Maybe she should extinguish a few candles, she thought desperately.

"And what is this?" Drake exclaimed mockingly. "Why, could it be…?" He stepped closer to the bar and set a bottle of wine on it. "Jiffy Cheez!" Holding up the can, he kissed it.

Blair smiled weakly.

"My favorite." Drake immediately began sculpting animals on the crackers Blair had arranged.

"I should have brought flowers," he said. "But this will have to do."

He held out a cracker with a perfectly formed rosette on it.

Just like the first time, so long... Okay, it was the day before yesterday. She felt sentimental anyway.

Blair stepped forward and Drake froze.

Puzzled, Blair stopped walking. When he said nothing, she nervously looked over her shoulder. "What is it?"

"Nothing." His voice cracked. He cleared his throat. "You look great."

"No, you look great," she corrected and accepted the cracker. "*I* managed to find a change of clothing." She popped the cracker into her mouth.

"I see that. Good job." He turned and concentrated on his animal sculptures.

Blair stopped chewing and just stared, stared at the newly revealed jaw of the gorgeous man she'd invited to dinner in his home with his food.

The same man who had appeared in the kitchen for two mornings in a row wearing nothing but a towel, and a skimpy towel, at that.

She squeaked.

He looked up. "You thirsty?"

She nodded, though she was content to simply drink in the sight of him.

"I have a lovely white wine here that should

complement the Jiffy Cheez." Drake walked behind the bar. "Corkscrew?" he asked and Blair tried to remember where she'd put it.

"Never mind," he said. "There are only two drawers. Wait a minute, here it is," he said holding one up. Now, wineglasses could be a problem. The shelf holding them collapsed and I think they all broke."

"Not all." Blair found her voice. "I found some in the back of the kitchen cabinets." She walked to the table she'd set in front of the open window. "I put two on the table."

With a dramatic gesture, Drake pulled out the cork.

He was waiting for her to return with the glasses. Blair could hardly function. She reached for a wineglass and noticed that her hand trembled.

It was her left hand. Forty-eight hours ago, another man's diamond—a faux diamond from a faux man, as it turned out—had graced her fourth finger. She'd been ready to link her life with his. She would have been his wife and would have borne his children, which would have meant sleeping with him. She'd mentally glossed over the sleeping part and had convinced herself that this was what she'd always wanted.

And now all she wanted was for the man behind the bar to find her one-tenth as attractive as she found him.

"Blair," she murmured to herself, grabbing the glasses. "You are one shallow woman."

MAYBE IT HAD BEEN a trick of the light.

Drake concentrated on removing the cork from

the corkscrew and not looking at Blair.

But he couldn't help himself. Those pants she wore might have been painted on. There wasn't room for a freckle underneath. Or lace. He was fairly certain lace would have been outlined.

There was no lace.

She was walking toward him.

Don't look.

But he did.

A revealing jiggle accompanied each step. Two dark shadows touched the white shirt, no matter what light she stood in.

How the hell was he supposed to sit across the table and make idle conversation with her? How was he supposed to maintain eye contact?

She arrived at the bar in a shampoo-scented cloud. "Here are the glasses."

"And here is the wine." How wonderfully witty he was.

Drake poured and they ate the cheese and crackers. He kept the bar between them until Blair moved closer and leaned her elbows on it as she talked. He caught himself losing eye contact.

"Shall I get more crackers?" she asked.

"No. If I want more cheese, I'll just..." He squirted an elephant onto the back of his hand.

Laughing, Blair held out hers. "I want a monkey."

Drake obliged, smiling. Then Blair licked off her monkey and he nearly lost it.

Remember her managing ways. Remember how she rearranged everything. Remember how much you craved your solitude. Remember that she's holding your Jiffy Cheez hostage. "This place looks great," he said. He'd have to order more emergency candles.

She perked up. "I hope you don't mind." She laughed self-consciously and tucked a lock of hair behind her ear. "I got carried away with the candles."

"It looks perfect." *You look perfect.*

She smiled. "I guess I should finish cooking dinner."

Drake gestured for her to precede him down the hall. Yes, it was so he could watch her walk. So sue him. "I smelled something wonderful as I came through the kitchen."

"I baked a peach pie. I hope it turns out."

"A peach pie?" He hadn't eaten a pie in ages. It had never occurred to him to try to make one. "I'm being overrun with peaches, as I guess you noticed."

"But they're the best peaches in the world," she said.

When they got to the kitchen, Blair removed the pie from the oven and Drake wanted to kiss her. Just for the pie, of course. Not because they were very much alone and she wasn't wearing underwear.

He was just going to have to get past that. Maybe if he ate a lot of food, he'd be too miserable or too sleepy to think about Blair and her bouncy curves and her long legs and her blue eyes and her fresh face and the wide mouth with the sexy brackets.

And then again, maybe not.

HE WAS SO GOOD-LOOKING, he made her nervous. Blair found it very difficult to refrain from inane babbling, especially since Drake gazed directly into her eyes as though he was truly interested in what she said.

She drank her first glass of wine too quickly and forced herself barely to sip at the second.

"Don't you like it?" Drake asked, gesturing to the bottle in the champagne bucket standing next to the table. Dry ice and water bubbled and set a romantic fog swirling down the sides.

"Oh, it's lovely. I wonder if I've had it before. Armand liked wines and I wrote down the ones—" She broke off. *Babbling, babbling.*

"And I'll bet you've got the list with you, too."

Blair slid a glance to her saltwater-damaged planner on the table where she'd been working. "Yes," she admitted, staring at her hands in her lap.

"You'll have to bring it and take a look at the cellar here," he continued, apparently not thinking anything was unusual about Blair and her list of wines. "I haven't studied all the ins and outs of wines. The owners just left the bottles here and I have no idea what I've got."

"Okay." Blair looked up gratefully, but Drake was looking at his plate. She let her face relax for a few seconds.

He's gorgeous and he's still speaking to you. You haven't run him off yet and you haven't spilled any food. The night is going well. Then again, the night is still young.

"The fish is great, but these—" he held up a

corn-bread muffin "—these are excellent, especially slathered with far too much butter."

She giggled. Ack. "Thanks. They're not hard to make."

"You'll have to show me how. I miss bread between supply runs. It doesn't last more than a few days because of the humidity."

"If you ordered yeast next time, you could make your own bread."

"Bread." He gazed out at the night just beyond the edges of candlelight. "Bread takes time. I've got time. Sounds good."

The smile he gave her, warm and approving, made tears sting her eyes.

This was not good. She was feeling things she shouldn't be feeling.

She was so easily manipulated, she thought with disgust. Let a man gaze intently into her eyes and ask her a few questions about herself and she was ready to…ready to…she didn't want to contemplate what she was ready to do.

She needed a break. "I'll go get the pie now."

NICE REAR CHASSIS.

Drake watched until Blair was out of sight, then slowly lowered his head to the table and closed his eyes.

His eyes hurt from staring into her eyes so he wouldn't start concentrating on his peripheral vision.

He'd talked about the most idiotic things. *Baking bread.* Although the more he thought about it, homemade bread might be the missing ingredient to his quest for the perfect bacon, lettuce and tomato sandwich.

Even the thought of the perfect BLT didn't squelch the things he was feeling that he definitely shouldn't be feeling.

She'd be gone in a couple of weeks and he'd never see her again. That could be a good thing, if all parties were equal and all parties were agreed.

But they weren't equal. She was here by accident and was dependent on him for everything. Therefore, the rules of love and war clearly stated that he shouldn't take advantage or indicate that he wanted to take advantage.

It was complicated when he tried to analyze his situation, but the main drift was "hands off." The "eyes-off" part he'd added all on his own.

He sat up and emptied the last of the wine into his glass. Good as it was, the wine wouldn't go with peach pie.

"It's still pretty warm." Blair had arrived, looking flushed and lovely and bouncy.

While he was waiting, Drake had cleared away the dishes, stacking them on the bar. Blair set the pie on the table and handed Drake the pie server. "How big a piece do you want?"

Drake looked from the pie, warm and waiting, to her. "I want it all," he replied.

She laughed and rested her elbows on the table. "You think you can handle it?"

"Oh, yes. It's been a long time since I've had pie. I didn't even miss pie until—" he gestured "—now."

"Go ahead. Have some." Her voice was breathy and eager.

"I'd like to. Believe me, I can hardly wait, but sometimes the anticipation is just as enjoyable." He smiled, allowing himself a quick lack of eye contact.

"I know," she said. "When it's cooking, I can hardly wait, myself. And you know the worst part?"

"*Is* there a worst part?"

She nodded. "It's when you've taken the pie out of the oven and you're waiting for it to cool. I'm ready for it, but I can't have it. Drives me nuts."

Drake gave her a slow smile. "That's why I always keep my pies warm. Cool pies aren't nearly as enjoyable."

"But if they're too warm, the juices run."

"Running juices has never been a problem for me," Drake told her.

Her lips parted. "You must have incredible self-control."

"I do," he assured her.

"Sometimes I just lose control." Blair broke off a piece of crust and popped it into her mouth.

"I know exactly what you mean." Drake leaned forward. "Just the thought of those warm, soft peaches in their sweet juice and the way they taste and feel on my tongue…"

Blair's eyes were glazed. Sweat beaded her nose. "I hope this pie lives up to your expectations."

"It would—will," he corrected. "It will." With a deep breath, he picked up the pie server and sliced into the pie. Cutting a wedge, he put it on a plate.

"I thought you wanted it all," Blair asked as he cut a second piece.

"I do, but I've found that...*pie* is much better shared." He speared a peach on a fork and offered it to her.

Blair smiled uncertainly before allowing Drake to feed her the fruit.

He was going to pay for this, he thought, watching her lick her lips.

MAYBE THE WAY to a man's heart really was through his stomach, Blair thought. He certainly liked pie.

"What happened that made you want to come here?" she asked.

Drake was midway through his second piece of pie and looking mellow, so she decided she had a fair chance of getting the answer to her question.

She knew at once she'd overestimated the quality of her baking. Drake dropped the fork and gazed hard at her.

"I don't want to talk about it."

"I can tell. Lighten up."

"Leave it alone, Blair."

"I've told you all about my stupidity with Armand. I'm entitled to hear your story." She sat back and crossed her arms.

"Why?"

She tried to think of a compelling reason. "Why not?"

"I'll tell you why not. Because I've had it up to *here*—" he slashed across his neck "—with trying to explain my reasons to people and having them tell me I'm crazy. I'm not crazy," he said, and Blair detected a wildness in his eyes.

"I'm not having a midlife crisis—or maybe I am, but it's *my* midlife crisis. For the first thirty-five years of my life I was a dutiful son, a great big brother and a valuable partner. But I was a hell of a husband."

"You're married?" Blair's eyes widened. She'd been lusting after a married man. Was still lusting, in fact. She'd sunk even lower than she'd thought.

"Not anymore and not for very long. But I married because it was expected of me. Don't get me wrong, I loved Tiffany—"

"*Tiffany?* You were married to a woman named Tiffany?"

"Hey, she's a terrific lady. I was the one who screwed up our marriage. Fortunately, she found somebody else, by all accounts a great guy, and she doesn't hate me. In fact, I manage, or rather I managed, their kids' college fund."

"Sorry."

He brushed away her apology. "I shouldn't have jumped on you."

"Do you still love her?"

He smiled briefly. "Not that way. The fires are out. We got married right out of school and I got a terrific job that sucked me in. She wanted me around more. She wanted to have a baby. Roger and I wanted to start a business. I chose Roger. Tiffany very wisely, but not very quietly, left."

Blair nodded, afraid to say anything in case Drake stopped talking.

"Roger and I decided we were going to make a

potful of money, then chuck the business and live on the beach. Sounded great to me, so I lived the business. I thought Roger was living the business, too, but somewhere along the way, he found time to get married. We postponed our retirement. And Exeter-O'Keefe got bigger and the pressure got more intense and the only thing keeping me going was knowing that I could quit in a couple of years. Except—people depended on me now. Lots of people. I tried to cut back and guess what?''

Blair shook her head.

"I was trapped. I had no life. Stress was killing me. So I told them that the day I turned thirty-five was my last day as a trader. And it was.''

"But why here?''

"I'd been here once and wanted to build a house on the other side of the island. When I tried to negotiate with the owners, I found out the whole thing was up for sale. So I bought it.''

"Did they tell you about the damage?''

"They did and I didn't care.''

"Why aren't you rebuilding?''

He finished the last of the pie before answering. "Right now, it isn't an option. I used my liquid assets buying this place and Roger refuses either to sell the business or buy out my half.'' Drake grimaced. "He's convinced that I'll be back, and I don't feel like getting into a legal battle at the moment.'' His voice dropped. "But I'm not going back.''

"I-I've been thinking.'' Blair stood and retrieved the pages from her planner.

"Sounds dangerous." His words followed her across the room.

"I've formulated a plan where you can rebuild even without investment capital on your part." Blair deliberately chose words Drake would have used. She wanted him to take her seriously. "Repairs can be done in stages and you could take on a silent partner. When Pirate's Hideout becomes profitable again, you can gradually repay your partner, if you choose."

"Didn't you listen to anything I said? I don't want to rebuild. Why would I want to work so other people can enjoy themselves?"

"You wouldn't have to do anything. *I'd* do it for you."

"You? What about your own job?"

Blair cleared away the dishes and spread her plans in front of Drake. "I quit my job to marry Armand."

"You could get it back."

"No, I trained my replacement so she could do my job perfectly. And she's being paid less money."

"So find a new job."

"I did. This job." She tapped the papers. "I can organize anything, and I can organize the rebuilding of this resort. I bet I can even find you investment money. Or you, with your contacts—"

"My contacts are mad at me."

"Then I'll do it."

"No!" He stood. "I like things the way they are. I don't want people tramping all over my island. And if this place is rebuilt, people will come here to *visit*. Lots of people. People I haven't seen since second grade. Friends of friends. Cousins of friends. Oh, and clients. In-laws and bosses of clients. Even people jumping off passing ships."

Blair made a face at him.

"They'll come here whether or not they're invited, and short of running them off with a gun, there's no way to get them to leave. But leave it the way it is now, and nobody in his right mind would want to stay here. It's perfect the way it is." He placed his fists on top of the papers and leaned until he was inches away from her. "I want to be left alone!"

"I think you overestimate your charm."

Straightening, he visibly calmed himself. "Instead of poking your nose into my business, you should occupy your time coming up with a plan for yourself. From what you say, you have no home and no money. Once Mario lets you off in San Verde, what are you going to do?"

With that, he stepped through the empty window frame and walked out into the night.

8

ONCE MARIO LETS YOU off in San Verde what are you going to do? In one sentence, Drake had forced Blair to accept the reality of her situation. And reality was not candlelight, a handsome man and a peach pie. Reality was burned bridges and no money.

What *was* she going to do?

Ever since she'd arrived, Blair had focused first on Armand, then the police, then Drake. It was time she accepted the fact that no one was going to help her out of this mess anytime soon. Until she could convince some government authority— or one of the investors—to investigate Armand's scam, she had to support herself. She wasn't going to talk herself into a job supervising the rebuilding of Pirate's Hideout, either.

It would have been perfect. Blair would have had a base of operations and a fancy title to impress those who were impressed by fancy titles. Her accusations against Armand would have carried more weight.

And it would have been an excuse to stay with Drake, though why she wanted to stay with a grumpy, if gorgeous, hermit was beyond her.

But he wasn't always grumpy—only when

people interfered with him. Drake was a man who knew exactly what he wanted.

As she gazed into the darkness, straining to see a bit of bright moonlight on Drake's clothes, Blair realized she'd hoped he'd want her.

For a long time, she sat with the flickering candles, wishing that Drake would return, to tell her he'd thought about her plans and had changed his mind.

But he didn't.

From the look on his face as he walked out, Blair knew that he might never rebuild. With the size of the *Pirate's Lady*, he wouldn't have to. Blair could see him sailing away in the boat, drifting from port to port. That would appeal to him.

Drake was a man who'd checked out of society just as she was desperately trying to check in. A man who'd pulled up his roots when she was trying to grow hers.

Their lives were going in different directions.

So now what?

Now she needed a plan. Blair pushed the papers to one side and opened her agenda to a new, but equally bumpy, project page.

Goal, she wrote, then modified it with *short-term*. If short-term didn't work out, there wouldn't be a need for long-term. Short-term was to get a job. But before that, she needed a place to stay. And to get a place to stay, she needed money.

She started another column: *Assets*. Underneath that, she listed: ruined wedding gown, torn veil, small gold earrings, salt-stained leather agenda, one set of underwear, one life preserver, used. And one heart, bruised, but that probably wasn't an asset.

It was so hopeless, Blair's head dropped to her arms and she cried for the first time since she'd come to Pirate's Hideout.

But Blair never cried for long, and by the next morning she had a rudimentary plan, which unfortunately hinged on Lupe's assistance.

Blair had slept on the library sofa. She was pretty certain Drake hadn't come in to read last night. In fact, she didn't know where Drake was now and, frankly, she didn't much care, except that she wasn't sure how long the radio batteries would last and she didn't know how to turn on the generator.

If she had to, she'd figure it out.

Striding toward the rec room, Blair heard Drake's voice and decided to eavesdrop. Politeness and civility be hanged, her survival was at stake here. If he was talking to the dispatcher/market cashier, Blair needed all the hints she could get for ingratiating herself.

"Now, Lupe, I know you're there." Drake sounded amused, not frustrated. "Come on, I haven't talked to you in two days."

"Four," came the reply.

Drake chuckled. "You know how I lose track of time." His voice was low and caressing.

Blair bet Lupe was purring. *She* would have been.

"So what do you want?" Lupe sounded impatient, but there was no bite to her words. The woman must not be as gullible as Blair first thought.

"Have you heard anything concerning my refugee?"

"She still there?"

"You know very well she is."

"Ha. Figured you woulda strangled her by now."

"She's not so bad," Drake said.

Blair hadn't expected him to say anything nice about her, not that he'd exactly *raved*, but it was better than agreeing with Lupe.

"So have you heard anything?" he asked again. "Any missing-persons reports? Outraged investors screaming?"

Blair held her breath.

"Nope."

Drake exhaled, covering up Blair's sigh. "So how about the status on that carburetor?"

Oh, great. She was in the same class as a carburetor. Blair listened while he and Lupe discussed the part. She wanted to peer around the corner, but didn't dare since she didn't know which way he was facing.

"You want I should read your messages?" Lupe asked after Drake agreed to pay extra to have the carburetor shipped express.

"Anything new? Anybody dying?"

"No, mostly the same old, same old."

"Then don't bother reading them."

"Except there's more of 'em."

Blair heard a faint groan.

"This Roger, he's sent letters. Sent them registered and I had to sign."

"Thanks, Lupe. Sorry you were inconvenienced."

"Sent some express, too."

"Roger is impatient."

"And what about your mama? A mama wants to hear from her son."

"Then she should listen to her son when he speaks to her," Blair heard him say. "You know the cards I left you?"

"The ones that say, 'I'm fine. Leave me alone'?"

"Yeah. Drop one in the mail for me, would you, Lupe?"

"Okay. I only got two left."

"I'll send you more when Mario comes out here." There was a pause. "I don't suppose there's a chance Mario would make an extra trip?"

Please, Blair breathed.

"No. He's busy. He only makes the trips as a favor to you."

"He makes the trips because I pay him," Drake retorted.

"Well, that, too," acknowledged Lupe. "Hey, Señor Drake, if that part comes in early, you want Mario to come on out?"

"Sure."

"Then you got your order ready?"

Blair decided to make her presence known as Blake unfolded a piece of paper. She strolled into the rec room, as though everything was just peachy-keen between them, and propped a hip on the table.

Though he never hesitated as he read his list, his gaze traveled up and down her length. "A *case* of Jiffy Cheez," he said, looking directly at her.

"That stuff will rot your stomach. It's not natural," Lupe said.

"Right on, Lupe," Blair said.

"Make that *two* cases."

"Did you remember to order yeast?" Blair asked. "You could use more flour and sugar, too."

"Hey, Lupe," Drake said. "I want to bake some bread. What kind of yeast have you got?"

He could have asked *her*, Blair thought. "When you finish, I'd like to talk with Lupe."

Drake released the microphone button. "That's not a good idea."

"Excuse me?"

"I don't want you antagonizing her again."

"She's the *police dispatcher!*"

"Yes, but San Verde is a little more casual than most places."

"Oh, for—" Blair hopped off the table. "*Fine.* But you can tell her for me that she *is* representing the San Verde police and if she won't talk with me, then she darn well better find someone who will. Because if she doesn't, when I get off this island, I will blab my story to every newspaper, radio station and sleazy talk show in the country because *I have nothing to lose!*"

And that was as good an exit line as she'd ever delivered, Blair thought, stomping off to the kitchen. A person had her limits and Blair had reached hers. She'd tried to be honest and look where it had gotten her.

She reached the kitchen to find that Drake hadn't made coffee yet. And he probably hadn't planned to. Why? Because no doubt he expected *Blair* to do it.

Blair, the rule follower. Blair, the good girl. Blair, who always tried to fit in and never got it right.

Boy, what a sap.

Blair jerked open the cabinet, grabbed the percolator and slammed the door shut. Armand had offered to make her his protégée. She should have taken him up on his offer. Obviously, honesty didn't pay.

She *would* go on the talk-show circuit. See if she wouldn't. She'd be bad. She'd be outrageous. She'd be the sound-bite queen.

Blair filled the coffeepot and fired up the burner. "Boil!" she snarled.

"Blair." Drake walked into the kitchen. "If you're not careful, you'll break something."

"Put it on my tab!"

"What's the matter with you?"

She glared at him. He had the nerve to look great this morning. "Do you think you're the only one entitled to a tantrum now and then?"

"No, but I think you're overreacting."

"Oh, really." Hands on hips, she faced him. "Did you give Lupe my message?"

He rubbed the space between his eyebrows. "She…had a line at the cash register."

At this rate, Blair's blood was going to boil faster than the water. "I hope she treated her customers well, because that's the only job she's going to have when I get finished telling my story."

"Blair—"

Blair spanned her hands. "Talk shows. Radio

interviews. Tabloid sales. Maybe even a book deal. And I have nothing but time to plot it all. Lots and lots of time.''

''I hate to burst your bubble... No, actually I don't mind bursting it at all. If nobody cared about your story before, they're not going to care now.''

She smirked. ''It's called spin, Drake. It's all in the way I tell it. The media is a giant monster just waiting to be fed. And I'm offering a buffet!'' She held up her hand and counted off her fingers. ''I've got all the main food groups. Money, scandal, sex, small-town corruption, the little guy fighting against the uncaring government—''

''Back up. Sex? There hasn't been any sex. I would have remembered sex.''

She gave him a pitying smile. ''There doesn't have to be. After days alone on a tropical island, everyone will believe it anyway.'' Especially when Drake's picture was plastered all over the newspapers. No woman alive could resist him.

But Drake hadn't had any trouble resisting *her* and don't think *that* wasn't a sore point.

''I'll deny it.''

She laughed. Then she deliberately tousled her hair and pouted. Grabbing a handful of her shirt and pulling it so her form was clearly outlined, she spoke in a breathy voice, ''Well...what are two people to *do* day after day and night after lonely night...''

Drake stared at her. ''I'll tell them there was nothing between us.''

Blair wrung her hands. ''He...he said that?''

Her voice quavered. "But I thought he cared about me!"

"Blair!"

She covered her eyes. "I can't talk about it anymore." She broke into sobs.

"Blair?"

Blair dropped her hands, saw his expression and laughed. "Ha-ha. You see?" She continued to chortle. "This is going to be great!"

DRAKE GRITTED his teeth, his hands clenching and unclenching as Blair laughed and embellished her abandoned-damsel act.

"I never thought I was the type of man who slapped hysterical women."

She thrust her chin up. "Good, because I slap back."

He stared at her, at the defiant chin and the mocking blue eyes, then grabbed her by the shoulders, hauled her against him and kissed her.

The kiss was hot and hard, born of frustration, anger and suppressed desire.

Especially suppressed desire. Drake had fought to keep from thinking about Blair ever since he'd pulled her out of the ocean. But consciously not thinking about her made him think about her even more. All the time, in fact.

He supported her weight as Blair hung limply against him. No doubt shock was keeping her immobile.

Drake didn't want her shocked. He wanted her arms around his neck so he could release her shoulders and let his hands roam over her body. He wanted to bury his fingers in her hair and angle her head so he could capture more of her mouth with his. He wanted his fingers free so they could unbutton her shirt, except she was wearing a knit shirt and he'd have to drag it over her head and they'd have to stop kissing for him to do that.

Abruptly, Drake set her from him. But not too far.

"What was that for?" she gasped, her lips parted.

"To find out what else you did back."

"Huh?"

"Never mind." Though she still looked dazed, he lifted her arms and put them around his neck.

Angling her head, he kissed her again. She still wasn't kissing him back, but that was okay. She wasn't pulling away, either. There was a lot to work with here.

Drake slid his hands down her back and cupped her hips, fitting her against him. She relaxed with a soft sigh that ended with a tiny moan in the back of her throat.

Drake felt it more than heard it. With one tug, he pulled her shirt from her shorts. Skimming his hands over her waist, he lingered, enjoying the feel of her satiny skin.

Then he allowed the image of Blair in her wedding dress, accompanied by one of Blair in last night's outfit, to flood his mind.

He could touch her now. Drake unhooked the lace bra and splayed his hands over her back, sighing into her mouth.

Blair flinched.

Okay, he was going too fast. Drake rested his

hands at her waist again and nuzzled the side of her neck.

He felt her draw a deep breath and began moving his hands.

"What's going on here?"

"I'm kissing you senseless." He nipped her ear. "Not quite."

Smiling, he trailed kisses toward her mouth. "I'll have to try harder."

"Drake, stop."

He stopped, his eyes still closed, his lips a millimeter away from hers. "I thought I heard you say stop."

"I did."

"Did you mean *stop* stop or slow down?"

"Red light."

Drake swallowed. "When's it going to turn green?"

She didn't answer.

He lifted his head and met her eyes.

"Where are we going?" she asked.

He smiled. "I've always had fantasies about the beach, but my bed is big enough for two." He brushed his index finger across her lips.

"No, I mean after that."

"Anywhere you want. We've got almost two weeks."

She gave him a sad smile. "In other words, until Mario arrives, right?"

What she was asking finally got through Drake's lust-soaked brain. "Well, yes."

"I see."

"There's nothing for you here, Blair."

"There's you," she said, her gaze steady.

He shook his head. "I have nothing to offer."

She tilted her head, a half smile creasing the brackets by her mouth. "You offer clothes, food, shelter and some of the prettiest scenery around. What more do I need?"

He remembered saying the same thing to her.

Though the blood pounded through his body and desire weighted his movements, Drake unhooked her arms from behind his neck. "You need a commitment. You want to build. You want direction. I want to drift, unfettered, through the rest of my life."

"You won't always feel that way."

Drake put a finger over her lips. "You can't count on that and you can't count on me." Kissing the top of her head, he left her in the kitchen, just as the coffee began to boil.

SHE COULDN'T HAVE HAD her crisis of conscience a couple of hours later, oh no. Blair couldn't just feel, couldn't just be swept away. No, she had to think. Had to push for a pledge that she'd be a part of Drake's future.

Drake wasn't thinking of his future. He was living the moment and what a moment it was. Even now, three days later, she could recall the hot feelings he'd stirred within her.

Some things aren't meant to last. Blair's problem was that nothing in her life had lasted at all up to this point and she hated that.

Drake was right. She wanted to build. Wanted security. She wasn't the fling type. She should be grateful that he was the sort of man who wouldn't take advantage of her.

Even though three days had passed, she was still filled with regrets. Engaged in her daily ritual of gathering shells and throwing them into the ocean, she looked back at the lodge to see if Drake had left yet.

She saw him walking along the path toward the *Pirate's Lady* and turned her head so he wouldn't see that she was looking at him.

They'd been avoiding each other, coming together for stilted shared dinners.

Of course, after the debacle last night, she'd probably never see him again.

Sinking onto the sand, Blair relived her humiliation.

It was just that Drake had looked so handsome, sitting in the candlelight of the library and Blair was regretting her scruples and thinking that a couple of memorable nights might not be such a high price to pay for future misery, since she was miserable now anyway. She'd put aside the book she was reading and walked behind him.

She had to touch him and so she'd tried the old rubbing-the-shoulders ploy. For a while, she thought it worked. As she'd kneaded the strong muscles, Drake at first ignored her, then leaned his head back and closed his eyes.

And there was his mouth, just ready for the taking.

So Blair had taken it.

For the briefest instant, he'd responded, then twisted away.

"It's all right," she'd told him breathlessly. "I can handle it."

At that, he'd stood and shook his head. "I'm

not sure I can. Please don't make any further physical overtures."

He'd actually said "physical overtures." Physical overtures? He'd sounded like a sexual-harassment lawyer. Embarrassment and something else she'd never felt before made her scream at him. Then she'd stormed off, unearthed all the Jiffy Cheez and thrown it at him, can by can.

Expressionless, he'd caught them all, thanked her and returned to his book.

Blair had returned to cabana number one.

"What an idiot I am," she moaned, imagining how she must have looked, shrieking at him and pelting him with Jiffy Cheez.

He'd be glad to see her go.

She sat on the beach, traced circles in the sand and gazed out at the ocean.

When her skin began prickling from the sun, she knew it was time to go inside. She was hungry anyway.

Standing, she brushed at her legs, then squinted at the horizon.

A black speck that she'd first thought was a bird, then an oil-drilling platform, had grown larger.

Heedless of the threat of sunburn, Blair watched the speck turn into a dot, then a lump, which bobbed up and down.

It had to be a boat.

The supply boat. Drake's carburetor must have come in early, after all.

Blair felt chilled in the midday sun. This was it. She was leaving and she'd never see Drake again.

Never see Drake again.

Never.

She wasn't ready for *never* yet. She couldn't leave now. She couldn't. She didn't have enough memories stored to leave. She needed memories—lots of memories to comfort her in the dark days ahead.

Memories of love. None of this imagination, either. She wanted specific memories and she wanted them now.

It would have to be now, judging by the progress of that boat.

Blair started to run toward the *Pirate's Lady.*

To save time, she peeled off her shirt.

"DRAKE!"

Drake heard Blair's breathless approach from inside the *Pirate's Lady* galley where he was checking the electrical connections. "Coming!" he called.

Hoping she wasn't hurt or hadn't set anything on fire, he scrambled up the steps and peered over the railing.

Blair jogged down the path.

Drake blinked. Damn, he had a vivid imagination. He'd undressed her in his mind so often his sense of sight had started doing the same. And doing it very well. He could visualize her lacy white bra as clearly as though she was wearing nothing else.

"Come down here," she commanded, breathing heavily.

Drake hesitated, enjoying the rise and swell of her barely covered breasts from this particular vantage point. "What do you want?"

"You."

Drake gestured. "Here I am."

"Okay, if you won't come out here, then I'm coming up there." She began climbing the ship's ladder. "In fact, this is a better idea. We'll be more comfortable here."

"Comfortable for what?"

"For sex."

He was hallucinating. He must have spent too much time in the hot sun—except he hadn't been in the sun.

And then she was standing beside him and he was still visualizing her without her shirt and wondering why, if he had such a good imagination, he couldn't visualize her without her bra, as well.

And then he didn't think, because Blair was kissing him and this time he wasn't going to push her away. Since this was all a hallucination, he couldn't get into any trouble. Right?

"Blair." He clutched her tightly to him.

"We've got to hurry." Blair wiggled her arms free and pulled off his shirt without unbuttoning the neck.

"Ouch—damn it, Blair, what are you doing?" In spite of his vow, Drake pushed her hands away and freed his head from his shirt.

"Memories. I want memories."

"Of what?"

"Of what happiness is." She planted little nipping kisses across his chest.

"That sounds oddly familiar."

She gave him a frustrated look. "Please, Drake."

"You're serious."

"Yes!"

"So you're really not wearing a shirt?"

Blair looked down at herself. "Um, no." Quickly she unzipped her shorts and tossed them. "Now I'm not wearing shorts, either."

Drake closed his eyes. Blair. Blair was here. Here and nearly naked. There had to be a catch somewhere, but damned if he could think of it.

His eyes still shut, Drake reached out and his hands found the curve of her waist. Moving his fingers lightly, he explored her shape. Gooseflesh rose on her skin and he smiled at her response. Desire zinged through him, but he deliberately tamped it down, wanting to luxuriate in the sensation of her body against his.

She was damp from her run along the beach and her rib cage rose and fell. He skimmed his hands lower and cupped her hips, which she rocked against him.

"Hurry," she whispered, her hands clutching him.

"Blair," he breathed. He bent his head, knowing her mouth would find his, savoring the moment, breathing in the heady scents of sun, sea and Blair.

His lips had barely touched hers when Blair unsnapped his shorts.

"Get with the program, Drake."

"I am, I am." He lazily traced a finger across her parted lips, feeling her breath puff against him. "Be patient." He gave her a heavy-lidded smile and bent his head once more. "We've got all the time in the world."

She turned her head away from his kiss. "No, we don't."

"Why not?"

Blair tugged on his shorts, but Drake tugged back.

"Because Mario is on his way—"

"Mario?" he asked sharply.

She nodded. "Yes, I saw the boat, so I'll be leaving soon. I'll never see you again and I—"

"Hold that thought." Drake stepped into the pilothouse, reached for his binoculars and trained them on the horizon.

Blair used the opportunity to pull off his shorts.

"Blair! Stop it. This boat might not be Mario and—"

"Holey-moley, I've hit the mother lode."

Drake snatched his shorts back up. "Behave!"

"If I'd known you weren't wearing underwear, I would have done that days ago," Blair said.

"Yes, knowing the one you're with isn't wearing underwear has that effect on a person." Without waiting to see her reaction, Drake peered through the binoculars again. "I want to make sure this is Mario. Not everybody who sails these waters is friendly."

"If it is Mario, can we have sex?" She wound her arms around Drake.

"You want to have sex with Mario?"

"No!" Blair swatted his arm. "With you."

"And have your only memories of us together be of some quickie? I have my pride." He didn't want *his* only memories of her to be a hurried coupling, either.

"Drake!"

"Hang on." Drake stared, trying to make out the details. "It looks like Mario, but...he's got people with him."

Blair stopped kissing his neck. "How many people?"

"At least two more, maybe another." He lowered the binoculars. Cupping her face, he kissed her gently. "Blair, I'm flattered, but..." He shook his head.

Blair's eyes filled with tears. "I'm not ever going to see you again, am I?"

Probably not, and the emotions accompanying that realization unnerved him. He'd miss her. But would he miss her enough to ask her to stay?

He couldn't answer, either her or himself, so he lifted the binoculars again and tried to blot out the sound of Blair's sniffling.

"No!" It couldn't be.

"What?"

"*Damn* it!" Drake looked around for something to kick.

"Drake? Are we in trouble?"

"Probably." He rubbed his eyes and looked through the binoculars once more. "Oh, great. You better get dressed. Mario's got my mother with him."

9

IT WAS WORSE than that.

While Blair searched for her shorts in the vegetation, Drake identified the others on the boat. "What the hell? She's brought *Pamela* with her."

Blair stopped her search. "Who's Pamela?"

"You don't want to know."

"Yes, I do."

He started swearing again. "It's Roger! Roger's with them."

"Who's Roger? Pamela's husband?" she asked hopefully.

"Exeter. My business partner."

"Oh, right, you told me." She found her shorts in a clump of sea grass.

"So who's making the trades? Who'd he leave in charge?" After that, Drake stomped around and only spoke in four-letter words.

Blair had her own problems. She'd left her shirt right out there on the beach. This was just great. She was about to flash Drake's mother.

Leaving Drake behind, Blair jogged along the golf-cart path, hoping she could retrieve her shirt before the introductions. First impressions were so important.

When she found it, her shirt was a sodden lump and she could make out people on the approaching motor launch. Fortunately, she couldn't see the whites of their eyes. Blair snatched her shirt, then escaped to the lodge.

By the time she'd put on the white shirt from the other night, Drake had arrived at the dock and was standing, feet apart, fists planted at his waist, his stance clearly stating, Don't mess with me.

He looked great.

Blair elected to remain in the lodge. Guessing that the visitors weren't going to stay on the boat, Blair boiled water to make ice tea. Tea was such a civilized drink and she had a feeling civility was going to be in short supply.

Drake didn't have any lemon, but she picked some of the fresh mint that was threatening to take over his garden.

Then she stood at the kitchen window and watched the drama unfold.

As she suspected, Drake was not welcoming. And as she also suspected, about the time she added the tea leaves to steep, Drake was leading a small procession toward the lodge.

One man remained on the boat and unloaded boxes. That must be Mario.

Blair had no trouble identifying the hatted woman in navy and white as Drake's mother, or the younger woman as the mysterious Pamela, but there were two men. Drake hadn't mentioned two men.

Looking murderous, Drake stalked up the cracked asphalt drive and stomped inside.

The little group stopped outside. "Oh, Drake!" Blair heard an older woman's voice. "You can't possibly live here!"

"I can, quite comfortably, as it happens," Drake replied. "Are you coming in or not?"

"Is it safe?" a man asked.

"That depends on why you're here," Drake said.

"I think we should accept Drake's invitation to go inside," said the other man. After some hesitation, the others followed his suggestion.

Blair was still in the kitchen, and they were now out of her sight. She decided to eavesdrop a little more.

"Drake, buddy, this place sure took a hit." Must be Roger.

"Three hits."

"I told you it should have been inspected. It's not like you to invest blind."

"This is not an investment, this is my home."

"Whatever you say, buddy."

The tone of Roger's voice was so patronizing that Blair braced herself for the sound of a fist striking flesh.

Amazingly, Drake restrained himself.

"Mrs. O'Keefe, let me find you somewhere to sit." This was a younger female voice, faintly accusing. Pamela.

Blair's eyes narrowed and she moved closer to the door.

"Drake, there isn't any furniture," Pamela said.

"In here."

Blair guessed they were moving into the bar and restaurant area. Now she wouldn't be able to hear.

She diluted the tea and added chunks of dry ice to the metal pitcher. Unorthodox, but effective.

Blair set the pitcher on a tray with glasses and mint leaves, then walked down the hall, trailing fog behind her.

"...situation intrigued him," Blair heard. "And Dr. Farnham would like to talk with you."

"About what?"

A throat was cleared. "What would you like to talk about, Drake?" Blair assumed this was the doctor's voice.

"I don't want to talk."

"Then you don't have to," the doctor said agreeably.

"But, Dr. Farnham—"

He interrupted Drake's mother. "We've only just arrived. Drake must become comfortable with us after these months alone."

Blair hesitated. What an odd thing to say.

"Drake, you haven't said a word to Pamela."

"What are you doing here, Pamela?"

"Drake! Do you see how hostile he is, Dr. Farnham?"

"It's what we expected, Mrs. O'Keefe."

"Just what kind of a doctor are you anyway?" Drake asked.

Yeah, what kind of a doctor?

"Well, Drake, I'm a psychiatrist."

"Mother!"

"Just think of me as a friend," the doctor continued in a voice that made Blair want to shake him.

"Shut up!"

Evidently, Drake felt the same way. Blair decided to make her entrance.

Whether it was the surprise factor or the frothing pitcher of tea, her entrance was more dramatic than she intended.

Mrs. O'Keefe squealed and clutched her chest. A blond woman about Blair's age immediately went to the older woman's assistance. After the first shock of surprise, a knowing gleam entered the eyes of a balding, potbellied man whose hairy white legs extended from a pair of relaxed-fit Docker shorts. The other man, thinner and grayer, alternated his gaze between Blair and Drake.

Blair crossed the room and set the tray on the table where she and Drake had eaten their last wonderful dinner. Then she glanced uncertainly toward Drake, hoping for some sign of whether he wanted her to make herself scarce or offer her support.

Drake looked awful. His jaw clenched and unclenched as though he was grinding his teeth. He was breathing shallowly and was standing rigidly at the bar.

He was furious. Livid. And something else. Fear? Panic?

He looked as if he were about to explode. Blair grabbed a chair and carried it over to him. His eyes locked onto hers.

She took that as a sign. "Sit down," she whispered. When he didn't move, she rubbed her hand over his arm, urging him downward.

"Pamela—Pamela, darling, don't look. He's taken up with a native woman." Mrs. O'Keefe continued in a stage whisper audible to all.

Blair opened her mouth to protest, but Drake grabbed her hand and sat in the chair.

He wanted her next to him. Blair was so happy she forgot what she'd been going to say.

"Well, Drake," said Dr. Farnham as though he were speaking to a child. "Why don't you introduce your friend to us?"

"Why don't *you* tell me what you're doing here?"

Mrs. O'Keefe glanced at Dr. Farnham, who nodded. "Drake, we've been worried about you."

"I've sent word that I'm fine." He tugged on her hand and Blair landed awkwardly on the arm of the chair. Drake slid his arm around her waist. "You'll vouch for that, won't you, sweetheart?"

Okay, she'd play sultry island girl for him. It was for a good cause. Blair nodded and gave him a smoldering look.

"But you haven't answered any of our letters," Mrs. O'Keefe said.

"I quit reading them. Found something else to occupy my time." He gave Blair a look that made her heart beat faster.

Boy, he really had great faith in her ability to play the femme fatale, not that anyone else had shown up for the casting call.

Dr. Farnham removed a small black notebook from his pocket and scribbled in it.

"You haven't returned our telephone calls." Drake's mother was beginning to whine.

"There's no phone here."

Drake was still looking at Blair. The touch of anxiety she'd seen in his eyes was gone.

"I figured as much," Roger broke in. "That's why I brought you this." He crossed the room and handed Drake a black object. "It's a cellular phone."

Drake gave him a look. "I know what it is."

"You can hit the Brownsville cell from here."

"I don't need to." He tried to hand the phone back to Roger, but Roger backed away.

Blair hated the way they were acting around Drake, as though he were a wild animal that they didn't quite trust.

She caught Dr. Farnham looking at the liquor shelved behind the bar, then apparently making notes about it. Uneasily, she wondered if alphabetizing the bottles was a sign of a personality disorder for which Drake would be blamed.

"I would like to hear your voice occasionally," Mrs. O'Keefe said.

"But you don't listen to what I have to say, Mother."

"Not if you continue to insist that you're not coming—"

"Mrs. O'Keefe," Dr. Farnham interrupted with a slight shake of his head. "Tell me about your days here, Drake."

"I fish, I eat and I sleep," Drake snapped.

"Do you cook the fish first?" Pamela asked.

Blair gaped at her.

"If I feel like it," he answered.

Pamela gasped. Mrs. O'Keefe and Roger exchanged looks. Dr. Farnham made a note.

Drake regarded them with contempt. "Oh, come on, Pamela! Even you've eaten sushi before!"

"Sushi and raw fish aren't the same thing at all," she said. Now that Drake's mother had apparently recovered from the horror of Blair's appearance, Pamela stood and glided to a chair.

She was very pretty in her white shorts, pink-and-white-striped shirt with matching pink socks, wristbands and visor. Blair could have hated her, but since Drake didn't seem glad to see her, it wasn't worth the effort.

Blair caught Roger's eyes on her. Him she could hate. Tugging at her midriff, she inched closer to Drake.

"I notice that you have an extensive liquor supply here, Drake."

The doctor's unctuous voice grated on Blair's nerves almost as much as the implication.

"The previous owners stocked the bar."

"That must have been convenient for you."

"If you want to know how much I drink, then ask."

The doctor obliged. "On average, how many drinks per day do you consume?"

"Depends on if you count a bottle as one drink or not."

Blair nudged him. Drake nudged back.

Mrs. O'Keefe gave them a look of disapproval. "Dear, this is a family matter. Perhaps you could go brew something else."

"She's fresh out of eye of newt, Mother."

Pamela whispered something to Mrs. O'Keefe, who leaned forward. "Do—you—speak—English?" she asked loudly, her lips exaggerating the words.

Blair snaked her arms around Drake. "I speak ze language uf luv."

"And she speaks it fluently," Drake added before capturing Blair's mouth in a kiss designed to let everyone there know it wasn't the first they'd shared.

But it was by far the best one. He was solid and warm and his hands were roaming where they shouldn't be. Blair would have been happy to kiss Drake as long as he wanted, but she was bent at an awkward angle. She straightened to find Dr. Farnham writing, Roger grinning, Mrs. O'Keefe averting her eyes and Pamela gazing malevolently at her. Blair left her arms around Drake's shoulders and tried to imitate the smile of a sexually satisfied woman—a good trick, since she wasn't.

"I made ice tea for you. Pleez help yourself." Her accent was less island girl than gypsy fortune-teller, but no one called her on it.

"I'll have some tea," Roger announced. He poured a glass as the women looked on warily.

He downed the glass and poured a second.

"Be careful, Roger," Mrs. O'Keefe cautioned. "Do you feel quite well?"

"It hit the spot," he said.

"Good grief. Do they think I've poisoned it?" Blair murmured to Drake.

"Don't you wish you had?" he murmured back.

"I'll have some iced tea." Smiling at her, Dr. Farnham approached the table.

He was a little late demonstrating his trust, Blair thought. The women apparently decided Roger was going to live and accepted glasses of tea from the doctor.

While everyone was occupied at the other end

of the room, Blair whispered to Drake, "Why do you think they're here?"

"This is a competency hearing, Blair. I'm surprised you didn't pick up on that."

"If that's true and you know it, then why are you being so antagonistic?"

"Because they've already made up their minds. Nothing I say will matter. It never did."

The defeatist tone in his voice alarmed her. "Yes, it will. Be nice to Dr. Farnham and he'll tell your mother she's full of beans."

"Then she'll be back with another doctor. And another. As many as it takes."

At that moment, Blair understood Drake perfectly. She knew why he'd come to live here and why he didn't want to go back. It was extraordinary that he'd put up with these people for as long as he had. What did they want from him? Why couldn't they just leave him alone? "Couldn't you tell Mario not to bring her?"

"She'd find somebody else."

"Good luck. I couldn't find anybody else."

"You don't have as much money as she does."

"Iced—tea—very—good," shouted Mrs. O'Keefe.

"And you called *me* irritating," Blair muttered.

"I'd like to see your house, Drake," Pamela said with an encouraging smile.

"Yes, Drake. We'd like to see how you live," Dr. Farnham seconded Pamela.

"Oh, I don't know if I can bear it," moaned Mrs. O'Keefe, yet she stood with the others.

With ill grace, Drake waved around the room

as Blair wiggled off him. "Bar. Dining room. Damaged offices that aren't structurally sound."

He stalked off down the uncarpeted hall, which even Blair had to admit didn't make a positive first impression.

The others looked at one another. Blair smiled and gestured for them to precede her. "I'm unarmed."

An impatient Drake waited at the entrance to the rec room. "My bedroom," he said.

Everyone's eyes were riveted to the rumpled bed.

The library doors were closed and Blair knew they might go unnoticed. She looked questioningly at Drake and he shook his head.

He ought to show them the library. It was the only fully restored room in the whole lodge.

Drake's mother entered the rec room and stared at the furniture piled against the walls. She and Dr. Farnham exchanged another glance.

Roger wasn't saying much of anything in support of his friend and partner. Blair wondered whose side he was on.

"And where's your room?" Pamela asked Blair, a hint of challenge in her voice.

"I leeve in a hut in ze jongle."

"Oh." Pamela smiled brightly.

"But I get lonely in ze jongle."

Drake grinned. "That's why she doesn't sleep in the jungle."

"Drake!" his mother snapped. "There is no need to flaunt your affair in front of your fiancée."

Wait a minute. Blair raised an eyebrow at him.

He glared at Pamela. "She's not my fiancée!"

She better not be. Blair, along with everyone else, now looked at Pamela.

Pamela blinked, then clasped her hands together. "Drake? I...I can't believe you said that."

"It's true and you know it."

"But..." Pamela looked from Drake's mother to the psychiatrist. "I thought he cared for me!"

"He does, my darling girl. He doesn't know what he's saying." Mrs. O'Keefe patted Pamela's hand and sent a glance toward Dr. Farnham, who was dutifully making notes.

"Bravo." Blair clapped. "*Myself* couldn't have done better."

Both women sent her murderous looks.

DRAKE STRODE out of the room. "It's uncanny. Is there some script you women pass down from generation to generation?"

"Drake, *what* are you saying?" Mrs. O'Keefe said. "You see, Dr. Farnham? He's speaking utter nonsense. While they weren't formally engaged, there was certainly an understanding between Drake and Pamela."

"Yes, a *mis*understanding," Drake said.

"If you hadn't...had your breakdown," his mother said, "you and Pamela would have been married by now."

He hadn't had a breakdown, but he would have if he'd continued his old way of life any longer. "You're delusional." He turned to Dr. Farnham. "They're both delusional. I hope you're making a note of *that*."

"I'm making notes on many aspects of this situation," the doctor said. "Please proceed."

How was he going to get rid of them? Drake wondered. The situation had gone from absurd to annoying. He could feel his blood pressure inch up notch by notch.

He grabbed Blair's hand and started down the hall. "Thanks for your support back there, *buddy*," he said when he passed Roger.

Roger spread his hands. "Hey, I don't know what sweet nothings you whispered in Pamela's ear."

"Empty nothings." Drake hooked his thumb toward a door on their left. "That's the storeroom. The kitchen is this way."

"And organized superbly, if I do say so myself," Blair murmured. "Be sure and point that out."

Drake grinned at her. She was being great and he was a rat to use her to fend off Pamela, but if Pamela and his mother thought he was living with someone, maybe they would finally leave him alone.

They piled into the kitchen.

"Here's another good *buddy* of mine." Drake walked over to a greenish-looking Mario, who was sitting on a stack of two boxes and fanning himself with a straw hat. "How ya doin', Mario?" He accompanied his greeting with a whack on Mario's back.

Mario grinned weakly. "Oh, hiya, Señor Drake."

Don't "hiya" me, traitor. "How was the trip out?

Smooth and boring, or was there a little rough water?"

Mario grimaced. "It was a pretty rough trip."

"Ah, but there's nothing like the movement of a ship as she rocks with the waves. Back and forth, back and forth." Drake moved from side to side. "And you've got the return trip to look forward to."

The last vestiges of color left Mario's cheeks and he closed his eyes.

"I see you've got my supplies."

"Yes. Two cases of Jiffy Cheez."

"That's all you eat?" Drake's mother wore a horrified expression.

"Don't forget the raw fish," Pamela reminded her.

His mother sank onto one of the kitchen chairs and brought a hand to her forehead. "Have you seen enough, Dr. Farnham?"

The doctor joined her and Pamela at the kitchen table and began to murmur soothingly.

With a wounded look toward Drake, Mario scuttled out the kitchen door.

Roger eyed the trio, then ambled over to Drake. "This is killing your mother."

Drake's jaw set. His mother, he could understand. Even Pamela, he could understand. But Roger? How could Roger be a part of this?

Blair linked her fingers through his and he smiled at her briefly. She'd been so supportive. And she was in for a miserable trip back with this bunch.

"How did Mother talk you into this charade, Roger?"

"She didn't have to talk me into anything. I was wondering if you're crazy, myself."

"That's the same thing I wonder about you."

The two men stared at each other. Roger, with his forty pounds of extra weight, pasty skin and circles under his eyes reminded Drake of where he'd been headed. "What about our plans?" he asked.

"We were kids dreaming kids' dreams," Drake said. "And part one of those dreams was Exeter-O'Keefe. This is part two."

Roger shook his head. "Man, how could you walk away from it? We had a gold mine."

"I made enough gold."

"*I* haven't!" Roger jabbed at his chest. "I've got kids."

Yeah, and where do you find the time for them? Drake refrained from asking. "That's why I stuck around another five years."

"Look. I understand that you needed a break. But you've been gone for months." Roger gazed at him intently. "You've got to come back now."

"Back to sixteen fun-filled hours of stress a day?" Drake shook his head. "I'm happy here."

"Happy? How can you be happy? You're living in squalor with—" he gestured toward Blair "—her."

Blair flinched as though she'd been struck. Drake squeezed her hand, then brought it to his lips and brushed them across her knuckles. He could have punched Roger for the hurt he saw in Blair's eyes. He might still punch Roger before the day was over.

"Pamela's waited all this time for you." Roger

leaned forward and lowered his voice. "I think you've still got a chance there."

"You mean I haven't completely alienated her yet? Thanks for the tip. Blair, think of something."

"Drake, show them the *Pirate's Lady* and the li—"

Drake stopped her with a finger to her lips and a plea in his eyes. He couldn't stand the thought of these people contaminating the sanctity of the library.

He saw the understanding in her eyes and dropped a light kiss on her mouth. "Pamela isn't even in your league," he breathed next to her ear.

"*Drake.*" Roger glanced over at the whispering trio. "Come back. It can be part-time."

Drake gave a short laugh. "There's no such thing as part-time."

"Did you read the prospectus I sent you?"

"No."

"Have you read *anything* I've sent you?"

"Not in the last six months."

Roger made a fist and the breath hissed between his teeth. "Well, here's the deal. I brought a computer with me. A primo laptop."

"That's not the deal I want to hear."

"You can work from here," Roger continued.

"No electricity." The generator didn't count.

"It's got batteries."

"For how many hours?"

"It doesn't matter." Roger's breathing quickened. "I'll send you cases of batteries. I'll have them airlifted to you. Anything. But you've got to help me."

For an instant, Drake considered doing as Roger wanted, but they weren't working toward a common goal any longer. Roger wanted more. Drake wanted less. "Find somebody else, Roger."

"But you're the best. The clients want you."

"I'm not available. You were supposed to bring in some hotshot to replace me. I assume he or she is handling my former accounts."

Roger looked grim. "I thought you'd be back."

Drake gave him a long look. "I'm not coming back. Either you buy me out, or we sell the company. That's what we agreed."

Sweat beaded Roger's upper lip. "I need more time."

"You've had time!" Drake was out of patience. For months he'd kept a countdown calendar in his office. Roger had known exactly how many days he had to make plans.

"What if you'd changed your mind? Huh? What if I'd shut everything down and then you'd come back? We would have had to start all over again."

"I gave you fair warning."

Roger rubbed his hairline. "Everybody talks about chucking it all and becoming a beach-comber. Sane people don't!"

This time, Blair squeezed Drake's hand. He squeezed back.

"You know, Roger, when you and Dr. Farnham first got off the boat, I actually thought he was a lawyer and you were bringing papers for me to sign. It almost made up for the fact that you brought my mother with you."

Roger looked back at Drake's mother. The

group at the table was watching them and had probably been listening for some time.

Roger lowered his voice, "I've got a liquidity problem, Drake. A pressing problem."

Drake was disappointed but not surprised. "Then sell the company."

"I can't." He spoke through clenched teeth, his lips barely moving. "Understand this. If you won't come back, then you're going to be declared mentally incompetent and I'll petition the court to make me trustee for your half of the business."

"Thus solving your liquidity problems." Which must be enormous.

Roger nodded. "I see you still have a grasp of business fundamentals."

"Go to hell."

"I warned you." After a moment, Roger raised his voice, "Okay, okay. Don't get violent on me, buddy." He backed away, hands held outward.

Rage welled up within Drake. He stared at the man he'd thought was his friend as Roger gave the trio at the table some embellished story.

"Drake?" Blair tugged at his hand. "Can he do that? Can he take over your share?"

Drake exhaled. "Probably."

"Then you've got to stop this."

"Don't worry about it. Let them do what they want. I'll refuse to come with them, so they'll have to return with reinforcements. By then, I'll be sailing away on the *Pirate's Lady*."

"In other words, you'll let them drive you away from your home."

She looked so aghast that he traced the curve of

her cheek with his fingers. Maybe she could come with him.

Maybe he *was* nuts.

Dr. Farnham cleared his throat. "Drake, Roger tells us you have no interest in returning to the firm you two founded."

"No, I don't."

"Yet this firm was a significant portion of your life for years."

"Yes."

"In fact, you worked long hours up until the day you quit."

Drake nodded, waiting for him to get to the point.

Dr. Farnham cleared his throat. "Drake, this sudden change in your behavior and life-style, coupled with your antagonism toward the people closest to you, tells me that you're a victim of depression."

That wasn't what he'd expected. "I'm not depressed."

"He isn't depressed," Blair said at the same time.

Dr. Farnham's smile was both patronizing and superior. "Oh, but I believe you are. You exhibit all the hallmarks." He pointed his pen toward the cases of Jiffy Cheez. "Eating disorders, alcoholism, and, uh, the lack of fastidiousness in your personal appearance, the squalid living conditions—"

"They're not squalid!" Blair argued loyally. She'd dropped her accent.

"Not to mention the low-class company he keeps," Pamela added.

That was it. "Get out!" Drake ordered. "All of you, get out of my home."

"Drake." His mother regarded him sadly.

"I'm recommending that you undergo therapy," Dr. Farnham said.

"You can recommend all you want, but I'm not going back with you." Drake couldn't stay in the room with them any longer. "I'll be at the dock helping Mario unload."

He tugged at Blair's hand, but she shook her head. "You go on," she said, facing the group. "I have a few things to say."

He probably should stick around, Drake thought, then decided against it. "You sure you'll be okay?"

She smiled. "More than okay."

THEY IGNORED HER.

She might as well have gone with Drake.

"He's not cooperating," Mrs. O'Keefe fretted.

Dr. Farnham turned to Drake's mother. "I warned you that we might have to use restraint."

Restraint? What were they going to do? Tie him up? Shoot him with a tranquilizer gun?

Drake's mother nodded, a pained expression on her face. "Anything that will bring him back to us, Dr. Farnham."

"The business is suffering without him," Roger added. "You'll have to move quickly. I don't know how much longer I can keep it going."

What a scuzzball, Blair thought. While Drake was working those sixteen-hour days, what exactly had he been doing?

Drake's mother gripped Roger's arm. "You

know how grateful we are for your patience,
Roger."

He nodded and patted her hand.

Blair stepped forward. "As I understand it, Mr.
Exeter, you weren't supposed to keep the business going at all unless you bought out Drake's
half."

Pamela's head jerked toward her. Mrs.
O'Keefe's eyes widened. Roger's narrowed and
Dr. Farnham blinked.

"Isn't that correct, Mr. Exeter?" Blair
prompted.

"Drake wanted me to buy him out, yes. But you
don't just dissolve a business partnership on a
whim."

"This was no whim, as you well know."

"Who *are* you?" Mrs. O'Keefe asked.

Blair smiled. "Come with me and I'll show
you."

10

BLAIR WAS ABOUT to give the most important presentation of her life.

She'd shepherded the group back into the dining area because she wanted the spectacular view as a backdrop. A quick trip to cabana number one for her notes and she was ready to begin.

"Usually, I have more notice when I give a presentation." She handed an old Pirate's Hideout brochure to Dr. Farnham and to Drake's mother. "And I naturally would have made sure everyone had a copy of the materials, but we're being informal today, so if you wouldn't mind sharing?" she asked brightly.

Walking back to the bar as though she was wearing her favorite presentation suit—the fire-engine-red one—and expensive pumps, Blair pivoted and offered them her most confident, professional smile. "I'm Blair Thomason, formerly with Watson and Watson Management Consultants in Houston. I've recently started my own agency—" *very, very recently* "—and am still waiting for business cards."

"So give us one of your old ones." Roger snickered.

Blair opened her abused planner and pried a stained business card from the front pocket. "I'm afraid my materials met with an expected dunking," she said, handing him the card. "As you can see, the roof leaks in several areas." Of course that wasn't what had happened, but Blair didn't see how her unexpected arrival on the island would add anything to her presentation.

Roger's snide smile vanished. He stared at the card, then at Blair. Without comment, he passed it to Pamela, who snatched at it.

"I thought you were some island girl," Pamela said accusingly.

Blair gave her a pitying smile. "I know you did, because that's what you wanted to believe. Much more face-saving than the truth. I'm certain there's a psychiatric term for persistent self-delusion, isn't there, Dr. Farnham?"

"Yes. It's—"

"But that's not why we're here," Blair said quickly.

"Why *are* we here?" Roger asked.

"Well," Blair said, using a pseudoconfiding voice. "I'm hoping to avoid an expensive and protracted legal battle. Unfortunately, I'm having a difficult time persuading Drake that it won't be necessary. To do so, I'll need your help—all of you." She made a gesture encompassing everyone in the stunned group. "But especially, you, Mr. Exeter, as you have the most at stake."

Roger sat down.

"Drake is becoming very impatient and is ready to throw the whole mess to the lawyers. After having met you and listened to your opinions, I can understand why he feels that way." She paused, and Drake's mother glanced at the others uncomfortably.

Roger was sweating. Good. He deserved to sweat.

"Now, I don't want to wait on the outcome of a court fight."

Roger quickly shook his head.

"I don't know how long my schedule will remain as flexible as it is now and I would hate to turn over this project to someone else."

Dr. Farnham murmured in agreement until Mrs. O'Keefe quelled him with a poisoned look.

"So let me tell you what our plans are and then see how far we are from reaching a mutually beneficial solution to our problem." She paused to smile at them again.

Dr. Farnham smiled back, but no one else did.

"I'd like to draw your attention to the picture on the front of the brochure. That's the lodge as it appeared before the storm damage. Inside the brochure, you'll see the interior of the lodge, including this room. I think we can agree that Pirate's Hideout was a very exclusive resort. It catered to the burnt-out captains of industry. It offered elegant simplicity, quiet and—" Blair swept her arm toward the broken-out windows "—breathtaking scenery."

Everyone turned to view the breathtaking scenery.

A shadow appeared in the doorway. "The boat's unloaded and Mario is waiting." Drake took in the group. "What's going on here?"

"Drake, please sit down and be quiet," Blair said. "You know how I hate to have my presentations interrupted." She held her breath and hoped he'd let her proceed.

To her shock, he did.

Without a word, he took a seat behind the others. "Carry on," he said, and leaned back in the chair.

She was nervous with him sitting there watching her. She wanted to do well, not only for him but for herself.

"Having toured the lodge, you'll agree that extensive renovations are necessary." Blair outlined the damage and what areas could be salvaged and what couldn't. "Though without the report from the structural engineer, I'm only guessing, you understand."

Then, using the notes she'd prepared for Drake, she outlined four stages of construction. She mentioned the *Pirate's Lady*, too, and the cabanas.

She did not mention the library. For some reason, Drake didn't want them to see the library and, although the brochure referred to it, no one asked where it was. But, then again, no one was saying much of anything.

Blair didn't give them a chance. She deliberately overloaded them with the tiniest details, many of which she made up as she went along. She spoke until her throat was dry and their eyes were glazed. At last, Drake's mother asked the question Blair had been waiting for.

"But why hasn't any of this begun?"

"Naturally, Drake has made extensive repairs, but—" Blair moved in for the kill "—Mr. Exeter is holding up funding."

Everyone stared at Roger.

"I am not!" he protested.

"Drake, correct me if I'm wrong, but as I understand it, you purchased this island using cash to achieve a favorable price."

Drake nodded.

"And assumed that proceeds from your interest in Exeter-O'Keefe would be forthcoming. They have not and, therefore, there are no funds to begin construction. Drake has expressed his desire to have the island remain a private holding and so we are at a standstill." Blair closed her planner. "I've tried to get him to explore alternate methods of funding, but he refuses." She spread her hands. "There you have it."

"Well." Mrs. O'Keefe didn't appear to know where to look.

"Thank you, Blair." Drake stood. "I realize that you were at a disadvantage without your normal equipment and I appreciate your willingness to wing it today." His amused eyes met hers.

"I must stress that these are only preliminary plans, since there are so many variables." She looked pointedly at Roger.

He was staring at the brochure, his face devoid of expression. At her silence, he looked up.

"But I think everyone here can see the possibilities," Drake said. "Along with the obstacles."

"Well, Drake, if you'd only told us," his mother began.

"I did. Repeatedly." He drilled her with a look.

"He never discussed it with *me*," Pamela said.

"No one close to me could have been in doubt of my intentions to retire from commodities trading," Drake informed her.

He showed great restraint, Blair thought.

A grim-faced Roger stood and the two men stared at each other. Without a word, Roger left the room.

Dr. Farnham also stood. "Mrs. O'Keefe, this appears to be a legal matter, not a psychiatric one. I admit that initially I might have given more weight to your concerns than was perhaps justified, but I'm confident that after a few sessions, I would have discovered that Drake is of sound mind."

"*Thank* you, Doctor," Drake said.

"Not at all," Dr. Farnham replied, either oblivious to, or choosing to ignore, the sarcasm in Drake's voice.

"But…but none of this explains his hostility toward me and dear Pamela."

"I'd be delighted to explore possible reasons for your son's antagonism, Mrs. O'Keefe," Dr. Farnham offered. "And with counseling, we can devise strategies for effective interaction between you. Please call my secretary for an appointment."

Blair turned toward the bar because she was afraid she'd burst out laughing. In the mirror, she caught Drake's eye as he made his way to her.

He slipped his arm around her waist. "You were magnificent," he whispered, and kissed her temple.

Blair didn't feel like laughing any longer. She stared at their reflection in the bar mirror, at the handsome man standing next to her in an "us-against-them" pose, and wished everything she'd said about rebuilding Pirate's Hideout was true.

"How did you know the plans would appease them?" he asked.

"I showed them what they wanted to see, since they *refuse* to accept reality." She was having trouble with reality herself. Perhaps it would be best if she moved out of Drake's hold, which she did. "My strategy wouldn't have worked if Roger had already bought you out and you were sitting on a potful of money. So be careful. It won't work again."

"Thanks." He looked down at her, staying close, even though she'd reluctantly moved away. "I'm grateful that one of us kept a clear head."

And one of us is going to have to keep a clear head now, Blair cautioned herself.

Drake was looking at her as though she were Jiffy Cheez on a cracker. He made her insides feel like Jiffy Cheez, too.

No man had *ever* made her insides feel like Jiffy Cheez before.

"I had to do something," Blair said, trying to keep the thread of conversation going. "I couldn't stand the thought of you being forced to give up your library before you finished Shakespeare."

He laughed, but it was an intimate laugh, accompanied by an intimate look.

"Anyway, I owed you," she said a bit desperately.

"Not anymore." Drake's voice was low. "We're more than even."

Blair looked at him, very aware that she would be sailing out of his life in a very few short minutes. That was *her* reality. Words that would have to remain unsaid clogged her throat.

Drake stroked her hair and tucked a strand behind her ear. The feel of his fingers on her neck sent prickles racing along her skin. She leaned into his palm, savoring his last touch.

"I want to go home," Pamela announced. Ignoring Drake, she made an elegant retreat.

"I think my work here is done," Blair said. She and Drake shared a smile as Pamela was followed by Dr. Farnham.

"Mario's ready to leave anytime," Drake said.

Blair swallowed. That was a hint if ever she heard one. "I'd better get my things, few though they are." She hesitated, hoping Drake would ask her to stay, but his attention was claimed by his mother and Blair slipped away before she started to cry.

She cried anyway as she stuffed her wedding dress and veil into a pillowcase so Pamela and Drake's mother wouldn't see them, cried as she slung the *Salty Señorita*'s life preserver over her shoulder and cried when she snuck back into the kitchen to snitch food because otherwise she didn't know where her next meal was coming from.

Of course he wasn't going to ask her to stay. She'd made her conditions very clear and he'd made his equally clear.

The fact that she'd fallen in love with him didn't change anything. She'd just fall *out* of love with him.

Then Blair saw the cases of Jiffy Cheez and cried even more. But she didn't take a single can.

Disgusted with herself, Blair splashed water over her face at the kitchen sink. She didn't even have sunglasses to hide the blotches. Everyone would know she'd been crying and they'd guess why. She'd better start preparing a speech about the evils of mixing business with pleasure.

Watching from the kitchen window, Blair saw Drake give his mother a brief hug and then she and Pamela stepped onto the boat. He didn't hug Pamela and Blair felt cheered.

He didn't hug Roger, either. The two of them spent several minutes talking, and judging by the rigid postures of both men, they weren't patching things up. That would be a mess, but it wasn't her mess.

Blair couldn't delay her departure any longer. There was no future for her here.

Of course, there wasn't a future for her anywhere.

How had she, who planned each detail of her life so carefully, found herself in this situation? She'd learned a lesson, though. She'd never completely trust anybody ever again—not even herself.

Blair trudged toward Mario's boat, wondering if she'd have the opportunity for a private goodbye with Drake. One last opportunity for him to…

Honestly, she was as bad as Drake's mother and Pamela, wanting things to be a certain way when the facts indicated otherwise.

Blair stopped a few feet from the arguing men and dropped her pillowcase and life preserver in the sand.

"Thirty days," Drake was saying.

"You don't know what you're asking," Roger insisted with a glance at Blair. "Don't tell me she's coming with us?"

Drake stared at her, an arrested expression on his face.

"Mario is giving me a ride into San Verde," she said to Roger.

"But I thought…I mean, I assumed you two…"

"There's been a lot of that going around lately," she said.

Belatedly, Drake stepped over to her and slipped his arm around her waist.

Blair removed it. Continuing the charade hurt too much.

"Blair?"

"I wanted to say goodbye, Drake."

Without looking away from her, Drake said, "I'll be in touch, Roger. Now, give us a minute alone."

Roger was already walking backward. "Sure, buddy."

"Don't worry," Blair told Drake wearily. "I won't blow your cover. I'll tell them I'm coming into town to shop and meet with contractors and so forth. I'll think of something convincing."

"You can't leave like this," Drake said.

"And how am I supposed to leave? You've been counting the minutes until the supply boat would come. It's here. It's leaving. It's time for me to go."

Emotions Blair couldn't read flickered across Drake's face. Slowly, he raised first one hand, then the other and cupped either side of her face. "You don't want to leave."

With the way he was looking into her eyes, Blair could only tell him the truth. "No."

"Then stay."

Stay. He'd said stay. "Here?"

"Here."

"W-with you?"

"With me."

He'd asked her to stay with him. *Stay with him.* It was exactly what she wanted to hear. Hoped to hear. Joy flooded her with breath-stealing intensity.

And then, as though she needed convincing, Drake slowly lowered his head and kissed her in full view of the group on the boat.

Blair instantly forgot about their audience. There was something different about this kiss. It was a kiss of promises, not merely a kiss of the moment, the way his other kisses had been.

It was a kiss of commitment.

Stay here with me.

Blair wanted to lose herself in the kiss and the promises and the commitment—especially the commitment. She pressed her body against his, longing to feel his arms around her.

She felt a chuckle deep in the back of his throat before he lifted his head. "Is that a yes?"

"Yes," she breathed, and tried to kiss him again.

"Patience," he whispered. "Now, let's wave goodbye or my mother will never leave."

Arm in arm, they walked to the edge of the dock. "You can shove off, Mario!"

"Okay, Señor Drake!"

As Mario chugged toward San Verde, Drake and Blair waved. Only Drake's mother seemed to wave back, but Blair couldn't be sure, since her eyes were blurry.

"I guess they're really gone," Blair said when they couldn't make out the figures on the boat any longer.

"Yes." Drake picked up Blair and spun her around. "They're gone and I have you to thank."

"I can think of many ways you can thank me, but they all involve the same thing."

He lowered her, sliding her down the length of his body. "What's that?"

"Taking off your clothes." Blair tugged at his shirt.

Drake tugged back. "Oh no. Let's make this nice and slow. We've got all the time in the world."

"Okay. That's a great idea." It was a stupid idea. "A fine and wonderful idea." Blair untied her shirttails.

"What are you doing?"

She unbuttoned a button. "We've been standing in the sun and I'm just so…hot." She pulled the fabric away from her body.

"Yes, I can see." Drake's eyes glinted in amusement and more.

"Blair unbuttoned another button.

Yes, there was definitely more there.

But before she could learn how much more, Drake spun her around and swatted her rear.

"Hey!" She spun back around. "Just so you know, I'm not into that."

"I'm not, either. Neither am I into rotten food, which is what I'll have unless I pack away the supplies Mario brought."

Pack away supplies? She was undressing on the beach and he wanted to put away the groceries? "How romantic." Blair had obviously overestimated her charms.

"You'd rather I left the food sitting in the sun?"

"Well…yes." She fluttered her eyelashes.

Drake laughed and grabbed her. Bending her backward in a silent-movie clinch, he kissed her. "Oh, my sweet, I've been so terribly foolish. We don't need food. We can live on love." He kissed her again.

He'd said the "l" word. Blair quivered. It wasn't precisely in the right context, but getting a man to say it at all was half the battle. That meant he was thinking about love.

Well, of course he was. Wasn't that why he'd asked her to stay?

Wasn't that why she'd stayed? She already knew she loved him. He just needed time to get used to the idea.

Drake finished unbuttoning her blouse, kissing the skin exposed by each button. "Blair," he murmured against her, "I hope you like fish. Lots and lots and lots of fish."

She started laughing and couldn't stop. "All right! Go put your food away." Drake let her up. "This is the most inept seduction I've ever experienced!"

"I thought you were doing the seducing."

"I was trying to, but you keep spoiling the mood."

"I'll make it up to you."

"And I'll let you," Blair said as they walked back to the lodge.

11

SHE HAD NO IDEA what she was doing to him.

Drake could hardly think as he packed away the meat Mario had brought—or rather, he *could* think and his mind was filled with Blair.

When he'd stepped into the dining room and had seen her effectively skewering the whole lot of them, he'd wanted her more than he'd ever wanted any woman. She'd managed to discourage Pamela, placate his mother, neutralize the doctor. And Roger—damn, she'd made Roger sweat. As he deserved to.

Drake had let his frustration overwhelm him, but Blair had handled everything. She was brilliant and sexy and strong and he wanted her.

And she'd chosen to stay with him when she'd had the chance to get off the island. *Chosen*. She hadn't been forced here by circumstances and she'd known exactly what the situation was.

She accepted his life as it was and, for the time being, was going to share it with him. She wasn't going to try to change him.

And he was going to do his best to see that she didn't regret her decision for one minute.

They were about to embark upon a fantasy interlude others only dreamed about. Time would

stop. Neither had any responsibilities or deadlines or end-of-vacation timetables.

Their affair would end when it ended.

Blair was the perfect partner for him, Drake acknowledged. Nothing and no one was waiting for
her. She was completely free to choose to do
whatever she wished.

She'd never have to hack at the roots of an old
life the way he had. He envied her. She was free
in a way he wanted to be.

And he would be. He was closer than he'd ever
been.

Blair was just coming out of the pantry. Drake
caught her and kissed her a moment before she
walked past him.

"Now?" she asked breathlessly.

"No. I'm only reminding you what you have to
look forward to."

"How about reminding me in more detail?"
she asked.

He grinned. "By the end of the evening, I'll
have made love to each of your five senses."

"How about best three out of five?" Blair offered.

"How about you trust me?"

"I do." She gazed up at him and he wanted to
change his mind about going slow.

"So." Blair backed away and looked around.
"Shall I carry this into the bar for you?" She
hefted a case of Jiffy Cheez.

Drake grinned. "Can I trust you with it?"

"Maybe." She threw him a grin back and sa-
shayed down the hall.

"Ohhh, Armand," Drake murmured, watching her. "You made a biiiig mistake."

BLAIR WAS NERVOUS. The hand-trembling, butterflies-in-the-stomach, have-I-lost-my-mind nervous.

She'd hoped for mad, passionate, spontaneous-combustion type of sex that wouldn't have given her time to be nervous. She'd tried that, what? Three—four times today?

Most women would kill for a long, slow seduction and a man like Drake doing the seducing. They'd look forward to it. But Drake was a woman's fantasy and Blair didn't have any experience being seduced by fantasies.

Nightmares, yes. Fantasies, no.

Speaking of fantasies, where was Drake?

After they'd packed away the food, Drake had shooed her out of the kitchen. Blair had raided the storage closet for a change of clothing, had showered and ever since had been hanging out in the library pretending to read.

She couldn't stand waiting any longer and intended to find Drake and tell him so.

She headed for the kitchen. On the way, she passed Drake in the hallway.

He'd changed into the loose cotton clothes that looked so wonderful on him, and his hair, still damp from a recent shower, was combed back from his face.

He was incredibly, heart-stoppingly handsome.

"Hi," she chirped.

"Hello," he murmured in a seductive voice. "You're wearing my favorite outfit."

Blair looked down at herself. "Pants and a shirt?"

"Yes, but it's the way you wear the pants and the shirt."

Blair looked at him uncertainly. She hadn't been able to find another shirt in the right size and this one was too big. It had a tendency to slip off her shoulder.

She tugged at it now. "Uh, when are we going to get this seduction thing going?"

He studied her. "You're nervous."

"What, me nervous?"

"You, nervous." He put his hand on the back of her neck as his fingers slid under the loose collar. "Come with me."

They walked to the bar and Drake stepped behind it. He reached into the tiny refrigerator and withdrew a bottle of white wine. "The dry ice is mostly gone, so this won't be very cold, but—" he quickly removed the cork "—I want you to *slowly* savor this. We're not after drunken revels here."

Blair giggled nervously.

Drake gave her a look. "We missed lunch today, didn't we?"

She nodded and he brought out the crackers.

Watching him fashion his cheese animals calmed Blair. He gave her several and she gobbled them. "Feeling better?" he asked.

She nodded.

"Liar," he said softly. "But a very pretty one."

"I'm not pretty," she mumbled through the crackers.

"You're absolutely right. I should have said beautiful." He propped his elbow on the polished wood of the bar and gazed into her eyes.

Blair brushed cracker crumbs off her shirt, which slipped to one side, exposing her shoulder.

When she reached up to reposition it, Drake stopped her. "I like looking at your bare shoulder."

"Oh, stop. I feel like I'm in an ad for wine coolers."

"Hmm." Drake tapped his fingers. "Yes, I've noticed things are a little cool. Relax. Have some more wine."

"You're not drinking wine."

"I will." He poured a glass for himself, but didn't drink any of it. "I have plans for us. Do you want to hear my plans?"

"I don't know—do I?"

"Perhaps I won't tell you, after all. I'll surprise you. Do you like surprises, Blair?"

"Sure," she squeaked, draining her wineglass.

However, when she held it out for more, Drake took the glass from her cold fingers and set it on the bar.

"Come with me, Blair." He came out from behind the bar. "This is an evening for the senses."

He led her through the dining room, where he'd set the table, and stepped out the windows.

With his hand at the small of her back, Drake directed her to the overgrown hibiscus bushes that had been planted next to the walls.

Picking a bright pink flower, he tucked it behind her ear.

"They're beautiful," Blair said.

Drake smiled and picked a yellow one, which he trailed across her cheek. "What are you thinking?" he asked, his voice low and intimate.

What she'd been thinking was that yellow wasn't her color, but she couldn't tell him that. "I'm wondering what you're going to do next."

Drake picked more of the flowers, filling her arms with reds, oranges, pinks and yellows. "At first I was thinking we'd put the flowers on our table, for the sense of sight. But now I'm thinking touch and scent."

"Scent? They don't really smell."

"Ah, close your eyes and breathe."

Blair did so.

"That heavy musky scent is used in perfumes. It's very earthy and elemental."

But not very pleasant. She inhaled harder, then sneezed.

"You have pollen on your nose," Drake said, and flicked it away with his fingers. "I'm thinking of how you would look as you lay naked on a bed of hibiscus blooms."

Blair sneezed again.

"Perhaps not," Drake murmured as he led her back up the gentle incline.

Great. She'd bombed out on touch and smell. But she did think the flowers were pretty.

Drake arranged them in the glass bowl he'd put in the center of the table.

Blair laced her fingers together and cast covetous glances toward the wine.

Pulling out a chair, Drake indicated that she should sit. "I will serve you dinner," he announced. "I will cut each bite myself and feed it to you."

He leaned down, but instead of kissing her mouth the way she expected, he pushed her shirt off her shoulder and kissed the side of her neck.

This was it. Any moment his fingers would begin to work their magic and she wouldn't be nervous anymore.

But Drake stepped away. "I'll bring dinner."

Blair waited until he was out of sight, then she leaped from the table and ran to the bar. Pouring a glass of what was undoubtedly expensive wine, she drank it all at once, which was the way she wanted it to hit her.

She wanted to feel soft and fuzzy and romantic.

What she felt was queasy. She was eating more cheese and crackers when Drake brought in a tray.

"What's this? Don't you trust my cooking?"

"I was just...hungry."

He struck a match and lit the cluster of candles at the edge of the table. "Come here then."

"Shall I bring the wine?" she asked hopefully.

"Only if you don't like the red I've opened." Drake indicated the tray. "It's been breathing."

"Has it caught its breath yet?"

"Yes." Drake chuckled. "I found myself in a steak mood this evening. Mario brought potatoes."

Blair slipped back to her place and stared at the grilled meat. She wasn't hungry. Probably due to her nerves and too many crackers.

But Drake had gone to so much trouble. He moved his chair next to hers and was cutting into her baked potato. "What do you like on your potato?"

"Oh, everything."

"I have butter and fresh chives, but no sour cream," he said.

"Okay."

Drake set down the knife and gave her a considering look.

She gazed back, wondering what he was going to do next.

He leaned forward and stopped.

Blair braced herself.

Drake closed the gap between them and kissed her. He raised his head, looked at her again, then kissed her harder, parting her lips.

Blair closed her eyes and leaned into the kiss.

This was it.

Only it wasn't. But she could pretend until it was.

Drake stopped kissing her, but he didn't stop looking at her. Sitting back in his chair, he leaned his cheek on his fist. "You're not with me, are you?"

"I want to be," Blair said miserably.

"So…what? You don't like the way I kiss?"

"I adore the way you kiss."

"You *adore* the way I kiss. I like that." He leaned forward and kissed her again.

Blair waited for desire to well up within her. She kissed back.

Drake stopped. "You're still nervous."

She nodded.

"This isn't like you—oh, Blair." Drake's face

cleared and he took her hand. "Don't worry. I've got plenty of little foil packages."

"I know, I saw them with the toiletries in the supply closet."

"So you aren't worried about that."

She shook her head, feeling incredibly embarrassed.

"Hey." He stroked her hair and tilted her chin up. "Just relax and enjoy dinner."

"Okay." He was being so decent and understanding.

What was the *matter* with her?

Drake handed her the wineglass.

"I should warn you, I already had another glass and you said you didn't want drunken revels."

"I'm ready to take my revels any way I can get them."

Blair laughed in spite of herself.

"There. That's better. You haven't smiled all evening." He cut a piece of steak and offered it to her.

She ate it, meeting his eyes and concentrating on the taste, trying to feel sensual.

She felt silly, and after a few bites Drake could tell.

"Damn, I'm trying all my best material here and none of it's working."

"I'm sorry."

"Don't be." Drake cut into a peach. "I look on this as a challenge."

"I don't want to be a challenge!" Blair stood. "I want to be…spontaneously wanton."

"Spontaneous? But you like plans. Detailed plans." He offered her a peach slice, then popped

it into his mouth when she refused it. "I was woo-
ing you with plans."

"I know." Blair paced in frustration. She
reached the bar and turned to face him. "It
doesn't make sense, but I feel...*stifled* by the
plans. I've *never* felt stifled by plans of any sort. I
don't know what's wrong with me."

She grabbed the white wine and poured a
glass. It was actually pretty good.

"I guess this place is rubbing off on you. Plans
aren't necessary here." Still eating slices of peach,
Drake wandered across the room. "I was a plan-
everything person like you once, except my organizer was the executive size."

"I figured as much." She watched, mesmerized
as he slowly demolished the fruit. "Could I have
some of the peach now?"

Drake cut a slice and held it out. When she tried
to take it, he jerked it out of the way. "Open your
mouth."

She did so and he placed it on her tongue.
"Taste. Savor."

She did, conscious of his eyes watching her.

"Have you ever looked at a peach before?" he
asked. "Looked at its shape? It has a very erotic
shape."

As Blair swallowed, she tried to think of
peaches as erotic. "You don't give up easily, do
you?"

"Nope." Smiling, he leaned against the bar.

Seeing his smile, Blair began to breathe easier.
She expected him to be angry and he wasn't.

Lord, but he was gorgeous.

She sipped her wine and he finished the peach, then idly began fiddling with the Jiffy Cheez.

When he handed her the cracker, there was a heart with an arrow through it.

"Oh, Drake," she murmured. It was absurd, but she didn't want to eat it.

"I'll make more." He squirted hearts on the last two crackers.

"Now you're out of crackers."

"Hold out your hand."

Blair did, laughing as he put an orange cheese heart on it. She licked it off as Drake fashioned something on his hand.

"What are you making?"

"People, but I'm better at animals." He showed her.

"Well, if that's the way you sculpt people, no wonder. They're out of proportion."

"Says who?"

"Says me. That woman would never be able to stand upright. And as for the guy, well, in his dreams." She laughed.

"You think you can do better?"

"I couldn't do a whole lot worse."

"Is that so?"

She held out her hand for the can.

"Oh no." Drake reached over the bar. "I'm getting you your own can."

He brought out two more cans. "You're going to need a lot of practice."

"Oh yeah?" Blair grabbed one of the cans and shook it.

"No, don't do that, it'll—"

But Drake's warning was too late. Blair pressed

the nozzle and a glob of cheese shot through the air, landing on Drake's cheek.

After a moment of shocked silence, Blair started laughing.

"You think that's funny?" He wiped it off and licked his finger.

She immediately stopped laughing. "No, no I don't."

"Maybe you'd like a Jiffy Cheez mustache."

She struggled, but he squirted a line across her upper lip. He watched as she licked it off.

"Hey, some got on my shirt!" She wiped off the cheese.

"Sorry," Drake said. But he didn't look sorry.

Then Blair pointed her can at him and sprayed cheese all over the front of his shirt. It was spontaneous, all right, but it was also stupid.

"Blair—you're wasting it." He pulled off his shirt.

Hey, not so stupid, after all. His torso was golden in the candlelight. Blair was so caught up in the sight that she failed to anticipate his retaliation, and seconds later she was wearing a Jiffy Cheez necklace.

"I thought you didn't want to waste it."

"I have no intention of wasting it," Drake murmured, and proceeded to nibble his way around her neck.

Blair held her breath at the unfamiliar sensation of his tongue against her skin. Her head lolled back.

"Much better than crackers," Drake whispered.

"Much," she agreed breathlessly.

The cheese must have sprayed in a much wider

area than she thought because Drake found it necessary to kiss and nibble all the way out to her shoulders, her earlobes and into the vee of her shirt.

"Your turn," he said.

She couldn't. But he stood there, patiently watching her. Slowly, she positioned the tip of the can over his chest and drew a cheese heart over his. Then she stepped forward.

The rise and fall of his chest quickened. His eyes glowed with an amber light.

Blair touched him with the tip of her tongue.

He flinched and dropped his can of cheese.

She stopped to look up at him.

"Go on," he whispered, his hands resting on her shoulders.

Blair licked off the cheese, tracing the outline of the heart. Drake's skin was warm and smooth beneath her tongue and she could feel the muscles beneath.

She wished she'd drawn a bigger heart, but since she hadn't, she'd concentrate on making certain she removed every trace of Jiffy Cheez.

"Blair..." Drake clutched her shoulders.

When she finished, Blair looked up to find his head back and his eyes closed.

She'd aroused him. She, Blair the ordinary, had aroused this lion of a man. And she'd barely touched him.

For the first time, Blair felt the power of a woman who was desired by a man.

He wanted her. Maybe even more than she wanted to be wanted.

She was so amazed that at first she didn't notice Drake looking down at her.

His thumbs slipped beneath her collar and worked the shirt off her shoulders.

Her heart pounded so hard she thought the fabric must be quivering.

As the garment slid lower and lower, Blair's mouth grew dry and she handed him the can of cheese.

Without taking his eyes from hers, Drake slowly removed the can from her grasp and set it on the bar.

Another tug and Blair's shirt dropped to her waist. Drake's lips parted. "You can't possibly imagine how many times I've dreamed of you like this."

The expression on his face banished any qualms she felt about pleasing him. Warmth coiled within her and she drew her shoulders back. "You dreamed about me?"

"Constantly. Incessantly." He closed his eyes and inhaled. "In your wedding dress."

"That's kind of kinky."

"It was wet."

"Oh. Oh!"

He opened his eyes and she was stunned by the desire she saw there.

"You're beautiful." He nuzzled the side of her neck. "Incredibly beautiful."

And he made her feel beautiful. As his hands caressed her back, his tongue made circles around her collarbone.

Blair clutched at him as her body shot its entire

supply of mating hormones into her bloodstream all at once.

"What about the cheese?" she gasped, not at all sure she could survive the onslaught of sudden desire. Did people have seizures from this sort of thing?

"Forget the cheese. I want to taste you."

And he did, licking a meandering swath to her breasts until Blair felt boneless.

When her knees buckled, Drake scooped her into his arms and carried her across the dining room, out the windows and down the slope to the beach.

"See the moon?"

To heck with the moon. "Yes." Blair hadn't opened her eyes. She'd take his word for it that the moon was there.

"There have been nights like this when the moon is big and full and I've sat on the beach, listening to the ocean and wishing I could share it with someone."

"I thought you wanted to be alone."

"Not lonely alone."

"Oh, Drake." She sighed his name. "You're not alone anymore."

"I know." He set her gently on her feet. "I'd hoped we'd make love for the first time here."

Make love. Love.

He did love her, Blair thought. Though he hadn't said the actual words, everything he'd done had been showing her that he loved her.

He'd carried her to a nest of blankets and pillows he'd arranged at the edge of the line of beach grasses. Now he knelt and brushed away sand.

Then he stood and loosened the drawstring on his cotton pants and they fell to his feet. He stepped out of the pool of fabric.

Blair was speechless. The brief glimpse she'd had of him on the boat didn't begin to compare to the Drake who now stood before her. The Drake who very obviously wanted her.

"I want to see the moonlight on your skin."

But Blair could only stare dumbly at him, so Drake kissed her once, hard, then unsnapped her pants.

"They're so tight, you'll have to peel them off," she managed to say.

"No problem," he said, and demonstrated that it wasn't.

And then he was staring at her in the moonlight. Blair could only marvel that he wanted her.

"Touch me," he whispered hoarsely.

And she did, running her hands over his torso and down his lean flanks, thinking that if she hadn't stayed, she never would have had these memories. And her imagination could never have done justice to this moment.

Then Drake touched her and she stopped thinking.

He pressed her back onto the pillowed sand and covered her body with his, his murmurs mingling with the rush of the waves and the whispering sea breezes.

Blair lost her mind to the feel of his hands and mouth and the hardness of his body against the softness of hers. And always, there was the spiraling heat.

She loved the way his muscles bunched when

she drew her fingers across his back, loved the strength in his arms when he supported himself above her and loved wrapping her legs around him.

She loved him.

And when Drake finally joined with her, Blair knew that at last she'd found a corner of the earth to put down roots.

12

BLAIR MIGHT HAVE STAYED on Pirate's Hideout forever if it hadn't rained.

But it did. Three days of hard, steady, tropical showers.

Three days of endless dripping. Three days of dark rooms and dodging puddles on the floors. Three days of water, sand and debris blowing into every open window.

And also, three days of fabulous sex and a couple of nude walks in the rain. But despite the wonderfully sensual experience, Blair longed to feel completely dry again.

The library was the only room safe from the wind and rain, but because of the books, they had to keep the French doors closed and the room became stuffy.

Making love on the leather sofa didn't help and only made the room warmer.

Drake didn't seem to mind and Blair hated to complain. He couldn't control the weather, but...

It was when she was between books that Blair got her idea.

Drake didn't want to restore the lodge because he didn't want to attract people to it, so why not leave the outside in a shambles and restore the interior?

Blair wandered through the rooms, grimacing at the sandy sludge that coated the floors. Cleaning it out would take hours, especially the dining room.

All Drake needed to do was build a wall between the bar and the dining room. Passing boats would still see the yawning black windows and the overgrown banana trees, but the inside would be protected from the weather.

After that, Blair couldn't help herself. She listed all the repairs—minimal, in her opinion—to make the lodge truly livable.

And after the roof and windows were fixed, maybe Drake would consider some modest redecorating. For instance, the rec room could be made more "bedroomy," Blair thought, and happily dabbled in color schemes and curtains.

On the fourth day, the sun came out and the lodge turned into a sauna.

"I'm going to work on the *Pirate's Lady* today," Drake told her. "I've nearly figured out the carburetor installation. You want to join me? Maybe we can take her out later."

Blair had a pretty good case of cabin fever, but she resisted. "Tell you what. I'll bring you lunch. I'm going to spend the morning drying out sheets and towels before we start growing mushrooms."

"You don't have to. I send the laundry in with Mario."

"We can't wait for Mario. The storeroom ceiling cracked and rain leaked inside. You've got a lot of wet laundry."

"Okay." Drake seemed unconcerned. "Then I'll see you at lunch."

Blair tried not to feel resentful as she hauled out stacks of sodden, dirt-speckled linen. If Drake had known the size of the job, he'd have offered to help her.

As it was, Blair found herself bent over a wash-tub that had probably never been used for its original purpose.

With a little electricity and a new washer and dryer, life would be a lot simpler.

After stringing a clothesline and wrestling with wet, king-size sheets, Blair was ready for a break. She used that break going over her argument for hiring a carpenter. And as long as the carpenter was out here, Blair could think of a few more things he could do.

Drake wouldn't have to be bothered at all.

Blair would take care of everything.

Armed with her plans and her lists and a can of Jiffy Cheez in the lunch basket, Blair practically danced down the path to the *Pirate's Lady*.

"Drake!" she called.

Within moments, his head appeared. "I wondered when you'd get around to helping me christen the boat." He waggled his eyebrows.

"Mmm, maybe after lunch." Blair climbed partway up the gangplank and handed the basket to Drake.

He'd already dived into lunch by the time she'd reached the upper deck.

"Your BLTs are almost as good as mine." He handed her the other sandwich and bit into his.

"Thanks." Wincing, Blair sat in a plastic deck chair. "My back is sore from bending over the washtub."

"Makes you admire those pioneer women."

"Yes, but I never saw myself as the pioneer type," Blair said. "I still didn't get all the things washed. The leak in the storeroom is pretty bad."

"I'll have to take a look at it." He found the Jiffy Cheez and held it up, a question in his eyes.

Blair shook her head. "There are several leaks you'll need to look at."

He shrugged. "Or I can find somewhere else to store the linens."

"That might be more difficult than you think," she warned.

"Don't worry about it," Drake said, tossing the can back into the basket.

"I'm not *worried*." Blair set her sandwich aside. "I did walk around and make a list for you."

"That's my girl."

"It's...a long list."

Drake held out his hand and Blair handed him the list of repairs.

She'd save the other list—the one with alterations—for later.

"You weren't kidding when you said there was a list. We'll have to put out more buckets." He grinned and returned the paper to her.

Blair tried to smile back, but she couldn't.

"What's wrong?"

"The lodge is a mess."

"It gets that way when it rains. Then the sand dries and I sweep it out."

"If you'd fix the roof and put glass back in the windows, that wouldn't happen."

He shook his head. "It's not worth the hassle. And I'd miss the salty breezes."

Yeah, the salty breezes that left grit everywhere. "We could leave the windows open," Blair offered.

Drake laughed. "Then what's the point of putting in glass?"

"*I* would be more comfortable."

"So hole up in the library."

"The library is...cozy." She knew better than to criticize the library.

Drake popped the last of the sandwich into his mouth and brushed his hands together. "Want to see the engine housing?"

Obviously she wasn't going to get anywhere with her improvement campaign at this precise moment. "Okay." But Blair wasn't abandoning her campaign for a carpenter.

She followed Drake below and half listened as he recounted his adventures installing the carburetor.

"Sounds like you're about to get the *Pirate's Lady* seaworthy again." She crouched next to the opening in the deck where Drake had climbed down to the engine.

Drake nodded, his sun-streaked head below her. "One good thing about making these repairs myself is that I'll know what to do should I ever have a breakdown at sea."

"Look, since you've got enough to occupy you here, why don't you hire a carpenter to make repairs to the lodge?" She spoke casually, as though the idea had just occurred to her.

Not casually enough. Drake shot her a look. "A carpenter?"

Blair nodded. "I'll just hand him the list and you won't have to be bothered."

"I don't want a carpenter here."

"If you hired a good one, he wouldn't have to be here long."

Drake shook his head and grabbed some long silver tool. "I'll take a look at the storeroom leak, since you're so bothered by it."

"Yes, I am bothered by it!" Blair found herself bothered by more and more things. "Drake, I spent *hours* this morning hand-washing all the things that got soaked and I'm not even halfway through."

"I *said* I'd take care of the leak."

"But why not fix all the leaks? And add glass to the windows, while you're at it. Why not make the lodge weatherproof?" She should have stopped, but once she got started, she couldn't. "Then you could have the wiring fixed and run electricity from the main generator. You told me it wasn't nearly as noisy as the emergency generator."

"I don't need electricity."

"I sure could have used some for a washer and dryer this morning."

His mouth tightened. "I didn't ask you to do the laundry."

"No, but it needed to be done." Blair thumbed through the papers. "I haven't made radical plans. Nothing that will compromise your lifestyle, but living here will be more comfortable."

"I'm—comfortable—now," he said between pulls to tighten a nut.

"I'm not," Blair said. "At least not when it

rains." She couldn't even contemplate winter. The climate was mild in the South Texas area, but the temperature had been known to dip to freezing during the night.

"Sorry." He glanced up at her, then went back to fiddling with the engine.

Why wouldn't he listen to her? "Drake, I even found a way to completely renovate the lodge without anyone ever knowing from the outside!" She shuffled through the papers. "You'd have to build a wall—"

"Hold it. I don't want to renovate. You know that."

"The place is falling down around our ears. You're going to have to do something sometime."

"No, I don't. I've got plenty of space and I can live on the *Pirate's Lady* if I have to."

Blair fought down rising anger. "What about me? What about the way *I* feel? I can't live like this forever."

"Nobody asked you to."

Drake's words froze her heart. "What do you mean?"

"I MEAN THAT when you're tired of me and tired of living here, you'll move on." Drake was angrier than he let on.

He couldn't believe that after the incident with his mother, Blair—*Blair*—was trying to interfere with his way of life. "Hey. Why don't we stop arguing about leaks and go check the crab traps?"

"We're not arguing about leaks. You're explaining about me moving on."

Drake was disappointed. He'd hoped she'd be

around longer, but it was obvious that the end was in sight. "Blair, we both know this isn't permanent. It's great for as long as it lasts and then it's over."

She stared at him. "Apparently," she said with a catch in her voice, "only one of us knew it wasn't permanent."

They stared at each other and Drake saw the hurt in her eyes.

Damn. "Blair." He reached out and she flinched away from him. "I never said..." Had he? "I never meant—"

"You asked me to stay!" she cried.

"Blair..." Drake felt about as low as a man could feel. He wiped his hands on a greasy rag.

"But you didn't mean you wanted me to stay forever, just to stay and play." Her voice was filled with contempt.

"I thought you understood," he said quietly.

"I didn't then, but I sure do now."

"Blair, I'm sorry." There wasn't anything he could say that would make it right. "I wouldn't have hurt you for the world. But we want different things from life. I'm not willing to live the type of life you want and you obviously aren't content on Pirate's Hideout the way it is." Mutely, he gestured to the crumpled papers in her hand. "You've only been here a couple of weeks and look at all the changes you want to make."

"Not changes. Improvements." Blair stared at the plans. "I can't believe you don't want to repair the lodge just for yourself. Just for yourself,

Drake. You can do that without reopening for business."

He shook his head. "That would only be the beginning. Say I let you go ahead. After a while, you'd want more. Then it would be, 'Can't we have so and so come to visit?'" He shook his head again. "No."

"I don't know any so and so's."

He half smiled. "Anyway, I want to sail around on the *Pirate's Lady* now that I've got her running. If I had a big fancy house, I'd be worried about it while I was gone."

"Fixing the roof would hardly qualify the place as fancy. But if it bothers you, there are plenty of people who'd be willing to keep an eye on the lodge in exchange for living here for however long we—you'd be away."

Drake recoiled at the thought. Changes. He didn't want any changes. He'd finally arranged his life the way he wanted it. "You don't get it, do you? And I thought you, *you* of all people, were willing to accept me the way I am."

"So it's your way or no way, right?"

Drake nodded. He'd waited too long for his freedom.

"There's something called compromise," Blair continued. "Each person gives a little and both people get some of what they want."

"I don't want some, I want it all. I've had a lifetime of compromises. I'm ready to be selfish. I want to do what I want when I want and how I want. And I want to do it by myself."

"I see."

He could barely make out the words.

"So you want me to leave now?" Blair asked.

No, honestly, he didn't. But she was unhappy and he didn't want to be responsible for another person's happiness. It was over and they both knew it. "I don't think we'll be able to get back what we had."

"No," she answered shortly.

He gestured to the engine he'd finally fixed. "I'll be able to take you to San Verde tomorrow."

Instead of saying a frigid, "I'll be more than ready" or some variation on that theme, Blair's lower lip quivered and she burst into tears.

Drake was caught completely off guard.

"What's wrong with me?" she said, sobbing. "Why can't any man love me?"

Oh no. "It's not you, Blair. It's me."

Shaking her head, she hiccuped out something that sounded like, "Ar-mand."

Nuts. He should have remembered she was on the rebound. Now he felt worse than ever. What was the matter with him? Just because she was strong on the outside, he'd overlooked the fact that she was emotionally vulnerable on the inside. "What happened with Armand could have happened to anybody."

She sniffed. "You do realize how stupid that sounds."

"I meant that a lot of women get taken advantage of by men."

"Men are scum."

"Yeah, looks like you're right." He wasn't in a position to argue.

"Quit agreeing with me."

"Okay, most men aren't scum."

"Except you. You're scum. In fact, you're worse than Armand. *He* never slept with me."

"I resent being lumped together with scum like Armand."

"Oh yeah?" Blair scrubbed at her eyes. "Well, now that playtime's over, you're going to dump me in a strange town knowing that I don't have any money, no credit, no job, no place to live, no prospects—and I don't even have any real clothes. I could starve and you wouldn't care. If that isn't scum, I don't know what is."

"I care," he protested, horrified at the picture she'd painted.

"Scum."

"I wouldn't have left you without any money." How could she think that?

"I don't want your money!" She flung the papers at him, then ran down the gangplank.

Drake let her go. When she calmed down, he'd apologize and keep apologizing, not that it would do any good.

This whole situation just proved that he was better off alone. Look how he'd hurt her. He didn't deserve a woman like Blair. She had a lot going for her and she shouldn't waste her life with him.

He sat on the deck and let his legs dangle in the stairwell. For a while there, he'd considered taking Blair with him as he sailed. The *Pirate's Lady* was an awful lot of boat to handle and he would have been glad to have an extra pair of hands during its maiden voyage. He planned to hug the coast until he polished his sailing skills, and Blair could have hopped off anytime she felt like it.

Apparently, he was being as unrealistic as Blair. He knew how she craved a home. She was the perfect candidate for a life in the suburbs, not living on a tiny, isolated island.

Drake stared in the direction of the lodge. Somehow, he was going to have to convince her that even though the two of them weren't destined for a life together, she was still a desirable woman and would make some other man a wonderful life mate.

"I am scum," he muttered, and gathered the papers she'd thrown at him.

He read snatches of lists and time lines. She *was* thorough, he thought, and then his attention was caught by another list. *Flowers, musicians, trellis, groom.* Drake smiled. This was Blair's wedding list. Looked as if she'd marked groom off too early. He flipped over the page and saw more Pirate's Hideout plans. She was running out of paper and was writing on the backs of other lists and plans.

Her whole life was lists and plans and organizing. She'd be a great PTA president. He pictured her as a mother. Any less than three kids wouldn't keep her busy enough.

Yeah, he'd miss her, but it was time for her to go. She wanted to put down roots and this wasn't the place.

Idly, he looked at the backs of other lists. Hello? What was this? A list of traveler's-check numbers—Blair was incredibly thorough—but other numbers, as well. Account numbers. Drake had seen enough account numbers in his lifetime to recognize them when he saw them.

According to Blair's notations, they had to be Armand's accounts. She'd never mentioned having this kind of information. What else had she recorded in that planner of hers?

He considered the possibilities as he finished working on the engine. So she had Armand's account numbers. The more Drake thought about it, the more he itched to see what he could find out.

He gathered the remains of their lunch and started up the path.

"Blair!" Drake called as soon as he was within earshot of the lodge. "Blair, I want to ask you something."

He listened but couldn't hear a response.

"Blair!"

"I'm in the library." Her voice was muffled.

The library. Drake's heart started pounding and he ran down the hall. *Not the library.*

"Oh, for pity's sake! I wouldn't hurt the library," she was saying even before he appeared in the doorway. He felt ashamed that his first thought had been so obvious.

"Since I'm leaving tomorrow, I wanted to make sure I finished the mystery I started."

Her eyes were red, but she was pretending she was over her hurt. Drake exhaled. "Blair, I'm sorry. For everything. But I might be able to redeem myself."

She closed her book. "Not that it's possible, but how?"

"The back of these papers you left on the boat—"

"The ones I threw in your face?"

"Yeah, those. These numbers—" he pointed "—they're accounts?"

Blair nodded. "That's my old one and those are Armand's. They're probably phoney."

Drake studied them. "I don't know. They look genuine. What does chocolate mean?"

"That's the Swiss account."

He grinned. "Very good, Blair. Do you have any other notes about Armand?"

Blair shrugged and showed him her planner.

"Mind if I borrow this?" he asked.

"Why?"

"I'm going to fire up that laptop computer Roger left and see what I can see."

She stood. "Then I'll be in the cabana."

"No, Blair, you don't have to go."

"Meaning I don't have to go to the cabana."

"Right. I'll turn on the generator and run power to the rec room. You can stay here."

"Stay here *temporarily,* you mean."

Drake nodded, feeling scummier by the minute.

"I just wanted to clarify your invitation," she said in an icy voice.

Drake briefly shut his eyes. "Blair, I've already apologized."

"I'm only making certain there aren't any further miscommunications between us," she said, settling back onto the leather sofa.

She'd be singing a different tune when he managed to access Armand's accounts, Drake vowed.

IN THE END, it was almost too easy.

Drake was filled with contempt—both for Armand and for the investors he'd fleeced. Didn't anyone make basic inquiries?

He walked to the library doors and stuck his head in. "Did you know Armand's last name isn't in this string of names you wrote down?"

"Yes." Blair's voice was clipped. She didn't look up from her book.

So she was going to play it that way. "Just wondered," Drake said.

By using the cellular phone and the laptop, he was able to poke around in any number of financial institutions.

The first time he was asked for a password, Drake called out to Blair, "Did Armand tell you his passwords or ID codes?"

"No," she answered.

Obviously Blair wasn't going to help him try to guess Armand's password, so Drake typed her name and, to his utter astonishment, discovered he'd guessed correctly on the first try. What's more, Armand had used "Blair" as the password for all the accounts—except the Swiss one. Drake didn't have any luck there.

Drake used his own Exeter-O'Keefe authorization codes, which were still active, as he'd suspected, and promptly drained Armand's accounts. Then he created a new one for Blair and funneled all the money into it.

Triumphant, he marched into the library to tell her, but she'd fallen asleep.

It was then that he noticed it was dark outside.

Drake went to turn off the computer, but instead began cruising the financial web pages on the Internet, catching up on the news.

By the time the foreign markets were open, Drake couldn't stand it. He took a hunk of the money he'd recovered from Armand and bought currency futures with it.

Then he sat back and watched.

By dawn, he'd made a tidy profit. "I've still got the touch," he gloated to himself.

Drake got up and made coffee. Blair was still asleep. He couldn't wait to tell her what he'd done. She had a healthy nest egg now. She could make a fresh start.

Though he'd been up all night, Drake wasn't sleepy. How many other nights had he done the same thing and hated it?

Now he felt…exhilarated. And a lot less guilty.

Setting his coffee mug beside the keyboard, Drake logged on to the Exeter-O'Keefe computer.

Just how much trouble was Roger in, anyway?

Within minutes, he had the answer: serious trouble.

Drake scrolled through the accounts one by one. How had Roger managed to run a successful business into the ground in only eight months?

He'd made huge speculative trades, then had made the mistake of trying to make it back too quickly. He'd panicked.

Clients had been pulling out. The business was worth far less than what it had been when Drake left.

Dreading what he'd find, Drake accessed his personal account.

It was all but empty. Drake reviewed the transaction history, saw that Roger had frequently used the funds to cover margin calls, but that he'd replaced them. And then one time he hadn't, except for piddling amounts to cover the transfers Drake had made to the bank in San Verde.

Stunned, he watched the sun rise.

It was obvious he'd have to return to New York and do what he could to stop the financial hemorrhaging. It would be a long time before he could return to Pirate's Hideout.

If ever.

"I smell coffee," said a sleepy-voiced Blair.

"In the kitchen." He didn't turn around to look at her. He didn't dare. He was afraid he needed her, but he couldn't let her know that. Not now.

"Have you been up all night?" she asked.

"Yeah."

"And?"

"And I'm going back to New York."

"BUT I TOLD YOU I don't want your money!" Blair insisted.

Drake ignored her and propelled her outside San Verde's tiny bank and in the direction of the bus station.

"It's not my money, it's your money. I got it back from Armand."

"How?"

"I transferred it out of his accounts, that's how. The man used your name as his password."

"Really?" She looked pleased.

Women. "Here." He handed her the checkbook, account papers and an envelope of cash.

Blair ignored the cash and was looking in the checkbook. "I wonder how much of my money he spent—" She gasped, then clutched Drake's arm. "There's way too much here."

"I didn't know how much was yours, so I took it all," Drake said. "Justice, don't you think?"

"But, Drake, all the investors' money must be here, too."

"Then give it back. You've got a list of their names."

"I will." She looked up at him. "Thanks."

He shrugged, wondering what she'd think if he told her that she was now worth more money than he was.

"How long are you going to be in New York?"

Drake glanced away. "A while."

They walked in silence for a time, then she said, "Roger messed up big time, huh?"

Drake only nodded, hoping she wouldn't ask how big.

"Where will you dock the *Pirate's Lady* while you're gone?"

Drake thought about not telling her. "I'm selling her."

Blair stopped walking. "You're selling the *Pirate's Lady?*"

"Yeah, it's easier." He tried for casual eye contact. Mistake.

Blair was looking at him with far too much understanding in those blue eyes. Fortunately, she also understood not to say anything else.

"So." Drake shoved his hands in his pockets to keep from touching her. "The bus station is right down the street." He didn't trust himself to go any farther.

"Yes, I see it."

They stood in the middle of the sidewalk, both dressed alike in khaki shorts and knit Pirate's Hideout shirts as though they'd been to an exclusive summer camp.

Blair gazed at him steadily. He knew she wanted him to ask her to come to New York with him, but he wasn't going to ask and she knew that, too.

In the end, he gently kissed her cheek. "Goodbye, Blair. Have a good life."

As IF SHE COULD HAVE a good life without him.

Within a couple of weeks, Blair had tracked down each surprised and pleased investor and had returned the money.

She still had a hunk left over. A hunk she decided to invest. In a boat. How convenient that she knew of one for sale.

Drake hadn't told her much of what he'd discovered about Roger's activities, but what he had said let her guess that Roger had really blown it and Drake was riding to the rescue.

So Blair was going to rescue Drake.

She'd planned to give him plenty of time to take the money he'd get from the *Pirate's Lady* sale and start remaking his fortune. Drake was brilliant. She knew he could do it. But in the end, she only lasted two more weeks.

So, a month after Drake had left her at the San Verde bus station, Blair, wearing a new red suit, followed Drake's receptionist to his office. She'd given her name as the former Mrs. Armand Varga, figuring that would get Drake's attention, since she hadn't made an appointment.

"Blair!" he said when he saw her. "You have a wicked sense of humor." But he was smiling. "You shouldn't be here."

"But I am." And just in time, too. He looked horrible. Very classy in his suit, but his tan had faded and his hair was shorter.

But his eyes were dead. She shivered when she looked into them.

He came around from the desk and took her in his arms. "Am I allowed to say that I've missed you?"

"Only if you mean it."

His kiss nearly broke her heart. It was more desperate than passionate, as though he was trying to transport himself back to Pirate's Hideout.

"Oh, Drake." She sighed against his mouth. "Are you rich enough to go back yet?"

"I'm getting there." She felt him chuckle. "How did you know?"

"Because you were selling the *Pirate's Lady*."

"Yeah, that hurt. But I needed seed money."

"*I* had money you could have used."

Drake drew his finger down her nose. "That's *your* money. You should invest it in growth stocks and not speculate in risky futures trading or wild schemes involving slick foreign gentlemen."

She tossed her head. "Too late."

His face froze and he gripped her arms. "What happened?"

"I bought a boat," she announced, and watched his face to see how long it took him to figure out which boat she'd bought.

Not long. Leveling a stern look at her, he leaned

against the desk and crossed his arms over his chest. "You bought the *Pirate's Lady*."

She nodded. "Paid cash. Got a great deal."

"You bought my boat," he repeated.

"It's not your boat anymore. It's my boat. *Blair's Boat*. That's what it says right on the side."

He shook his head. "You shouldn't have told me you bought my boat."

"Why not?"

"Because now when I tell you I'm in love with you, you'll think it's because of the boat."

"You're in love with me?" She felt a goofy grin spread over her face.

He nodded. "Yeah."

"It's because of the boat, isn't it?"

"Come here." He opened his arms and Blair stepped into his embrace. "I suppose you want to hear me confess that I've been a blind idiot and all that."

"You betcha."

He sighed. "I...can't live here. I can't live like this. But I can't live without you, either."

"So let's go home."

"Home?"

She smiled. "Pirate's Hideout. I already put down roots. I couldn't help it. That's what happens when you fall in love with somebody. Home is where the heart is."

Drake ran his knuckles over her cheek. "You think you can be happy there?"

"With you."

"Exactly the way things are?"

"Certainly not," she said coolly. "I want full-time electricity, telephone and repairs to the lodge. I see no reason to be uncomfortable, but if you want to go native, there are six cabanas scattered over the island."

He blinked. "Is that all?"

"No. I have a list."

She unfolded a paper and he laughed. "I knew you would."

He scanned the list. "I can live with this. But what about you? Won't you get bored and lonely?"

"If I do, I'll just sail into San Verde. I've got my own transportation, you know."

Drake burst out laughing. "Oh, Blair, I do love you. But," he said, dangling the paper in front of her, "you're slipping. You left one very important item off the list."

"What?"

"Our wedding."

"Well, actually…" She held up a brand-new planner. "I wanted to be prepared in case I needed it."

"You need it," he said just before he kissed her.

"I need you," Blair said.

"I need you, too." Drake sighed. "But I've got to get back to work."

"Not until after lunch."

"Blair, I can't leave now."

"You don't have to. I brought lunch." She reached into her purse and withdrew a can of Jiffy Cheez.

"That's lunch?"

"Yes." Blair hopped onto the desk and tossed him the can.

"Where are the crackers?" Drake asked.

Blair smiled and began unbuttoning her suit. "I didn't bring any."

* * *

BRIDES ON THE RUN continues next month
with *Not This Gal!* by Glenda Sanders.
Don't miss it!

This month's irresistible novels from

Temptation®

THE BLACK SHEEP by Carolyn Andrews

Nick Heagerty was a loner, a rebel *with* a cause. Ten years ago he'd been accused of a crime he didn't commit—and he'd left town without a backward glance. Now he was back—but not for long. Then *everything* changed when he met gorgeous P.I. Andie Field and realized that his wandering days were numbered...

WISHES by Rita Clay Estrada

When Virginia Gallagher found a wallet full of cash, it would've been the answer to her prayers, *if* she hadn't been so honest. When Wilder Hunnicut came to pick it up, *he* would've been a wish come true, *if* he hadn't been out of her league. And when her reward was a lamp with three wishes, she started hoping wishes really could come true...

AFTER THE LOVING by Sandy Steen

It Happened One Night

To claim her inheritance, Isabella Farentino must find a husband—fast! The only man around is the arrogant, infuriatingly sexy Cade McBride. Belle's counting on his love-and-leave-them attitude to get him out of her life, but after one incredible wedding night with Cade, she's having second thoughts...

BRIDE OVERBOARD by Heather MacAllister

Brides on the Run

Blair Thomason was about to take the plunge—into marriage, that is. But when she found herself on a yacht, about to marry a crook, she plunged into the sea instead! Luckily, Drake O'Keefe was there to rescue her... She'd barely escaped marrying one man, only to be stranded with another!

Spoil yourself next month
with these four novels from

ROARKE: THE ADVENTURER by JoAnn Ross

New Orleans Lovers

Shaken by an attempt on his life, journalist Roarke O'Malley
returned home. But he was thrown into more danger when
beautiful Daria Shea turned to him for help. Without her
memory, she had no idea who was trying to hurt her or why...
And as they investigated together, the sultry days turned into hot,
passionate nights...

NOT THIS GAL! by Glenda Sanders

Brides on the Run

Keeley Owens was in a tacky Las Vegas wedding chapel, about
to marry her drunken boyfriend, when she realized it would be a
fate worse than death. So she stalked off into the desert—only to
be rescued by a gorgeous stranger. He wined her, dined her and
loved her all night long. But Keeley had only just left one groom
at the altar...

ONE ENCHANTED NIGHT by Debra Carroll

It Happened One Night

The man Lucy Weston found on her doorstep was half-dead from
the winter storm outside. She kept him alive with the warmth of
her body, and reacted to him as she never had to any man. He
was a strong, sensual lover. But he had no idea who he was...

ONE HOT SUMMER by Suzanne Scott

Jillian Sanderson had just inherited half an inn—but the other
half was a problem. Because that half belonged to sexy-as-sin
Kit Malone...and the fever that raged between them was
uncontrollable. Would Kit stay around if they could make those
hot summer nights last forever?

On sale from 6th April 1998

4 FREE

books and a surprise gift!

We would like to take this opportunity to thank you for reading this Mills & Boon® book by offering you the chance to take FOUR more specially selected titles from the Temptation® series absolutely FREE! We're also making this offer to introduce you to the benefits of the Reader Service™—

★ FREE home delivery
★ FREE gifts and competitions
★ FREE monthly newsletter
★ Books available before they're in the shops
★ Exclusive Reader Service discounts

Accepting these FREE books and gift places you under no obligation to buy, you may cancel at any time, even after receiving your free shipment. Simply complete your details below and return the entire page to the address below. *You don't even need a stamp!*

YES! Please send me 4 free Temptation books and a surprise gift. I understand that unless you hear from me, I will receive 4 superb new titles every month for just £2.30 each, postage and packing free. I am under no obligation to purchase any books and may cancel my subscription at any time. The free books and gift will be mine to keep in any case.

T8XE

Ms/Mrs/Miss/Mr...................................Initials ....
BLOCK CAPITALS PLEASE

Surname ....

Address ....

....

....Postcode..................................

Send this whole page to:
THE READER SERVICE, FREEPOST, CROYDON, CR9 3WZ
(Eire readers please send coupon to: P.O. BOX 4546, DUBLIN 24.)

Offer not valid to current Reader Service subscribers to this series. We reserve the right to refuse an application and applicants must be aged 18 years or over. Only one application per household. Terms and prices subject to change without notice. Offer expires 30th September 1998. You may be mailed with offers from other reputable companies as a result of this application. If you would prefer not to receive such offers, please tick box. ☐
Mills & Boon Temptation® is a registered trademark of
Harlequin Mills & Boon Ltd.

MARY LYNN BAXTER

࿇࿇࿇࿇࿇࿇࿇࿇

Raw Heat

Successful broadcast journalist Juliana Reed is caught
in a web of corruption, blackmail and murder. Texas
Ranger, Gates O'Brien—her ex-husband—is the only
person she can turn to. Both know that getting out
alive is just the beginning...

*"Baxter's writing...strikes every chord within
the female spirit."*
—Bestselling author Sandra Brown

1-55166-394-5
AVAILABLE FROM APRIL 1998

MIRA®

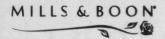
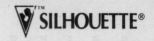

SPECIAL OFFER
£5 OFF

FLYING FLOWERS

Beautiful fresh flowers, sent by 1st class post to any UK and Eire address.

We have teamed up with Flying Flowers, the UK's premier 'flowers by post' company, to offer you £5 off a choice of their two most popular bouquets the 18 mix (CAS) of 10 multihead and 8 luxury bloom Carnations and the 25 mix (CFG) of 15 luxury bloom Carnations, 10 Freesias and Gypsophila. All bouquets contain fresh flowers 'in bud, added greenery, bouquet wrap, flower food, care instructions, and personal message card. They are boxed, gift wrapped and sent by 1st class post.

To redeem £5 off a Flying Flowers bouquet simply complete the application form below and send it with your cheque or postal order to; **HMB Flying Flowers Offer, The Jersey Flower Centre, Jersey JE1 5**

ORDER FORM (Block capitals please) Valid for delivery anytime until 30th November 1998 MAB/029

Title ....Initials ....Surname ....

Address...

....Postcode ....

Signature...Are you a Reader Service Subscriber YES

Bouquet(s)**18 CAS** (Usual Price £14.99) **£9.99** ☐   **25 CFG** (Usual Price £19.99) **£14.99** ☐

I enclose a cheque/postal order payable to Flying Flowers for £.........................or payment

VISA/MASTERCARD ☐☐☐☐☐☐☐☐☐☐☐☐☐☐☐☐ Expiry Date........../........../

PLEASE SEND MY BOUQUET TO ARRIVE BY........../........../

TO Title ....Initials ....Surname ....

Address...

....Postcode ....

Message (Max 10 Words) ....

....

Please allow a minimum of four working days between receipt of order and 'required by date' for deli

You may be mailed with offers from other reputable companies as a result of this application. Please tick box if you would prefer not to receive such offers. ☐

Terms and Conditions Although dispatched by 1st class post to arrive by the required date the exact day of delivery cannot be guaran Valid for delivery anytime until 30th November 1998. Maximum of 5 redemptions per household. photocopies of the voucher will be accepted.